# Coral Hearts

## The Morgan Brothers Book 1

### By Avery Gale

© Copyright January 2016 by Avery Gale
ISBN 978-1-944472-27-6
All cover art and logo © Copyright 2016 by Avery Gale
All rights reserved.

Cover Design by Jess Buffett
Published by Avery Gale Books

## Chapter One

CORAL WOULD RECOGNIZE the sound of his walk anywhere. The distinctive scrape of well-worn Ariat boots and the metallic clink of spurs against the hardware store's aged wide plank flooring left no doubt Sage Morgan was stalking down the store's wide center aisle. The man never simply *walked* anywhere. He was either stomping like an angry bull in a china closet, swaggering like he had the world in his pocket—which was pretty close to the truth, or he was stalking some unsuspecting fool who'd messed up his order. *Holy Mother Mary and sweet baby Jesus, don't let it be me—not today.*

Sighing softly to herself, Coral simply didn't have the energy to deal with Sage if he was aggravated with her. She couldn't remember making an error on his last order, but then again, she hadn't been getting enough sleep to remember much of anything. Coral tried to stand perfectly still at the top of the ladder where she was currently teetering. She hoped like hell he didn't notice her. The man was sex on two legs and her traitorous body reacted to him in ways that were downright embarrassing. Sage Morgan had the starring role in each and every one of her erotic fantasies. And, the more rumors she heard about his sexual predilections the hotter those fantasies became.

Even though they'd eaten lunch together a few times recently, Coral was sure it had simply been a matter of convenience in the crowded diner. She needed to remember he'd simply been polite, and it didn't mean he'd actually want to fulfill those hot porn clips playing out in her imagination any time she thought about him. Something about Sage Morgan tugged at her very soul and she wasn't even sure what it was about him that called to her. He was tall, dark, and intimidating, but there was a softer side to the shrewd businessman others seemed focused on.

Coral enjoyed their conversations, and Sage seemed to enjoy bantering with her as well. She'd been amazed at his wide range of interests even as they'd teased each other about differing opinions on a few things. Sage always listened attentively to her views and never criticized her even when he hadn't agreed with her. And damn if that wasn't just one more another thing that made him insanely sexy in her eyes. Knowing he respected her opinion warmed her heart—no one had ever cared about anything except what she could do for them.

For the most part, over the past year Sage had seemed content to just watch her from a distance—their interactions had been intermittent at best. She'd chalked it up to luck. It was as if she'd somehow acquired her own guardian angel in the flesh…and some mighty fine flesh she'd bet it was too. Rolling her eyes at her own sass, Coral tried to keep still as Sage drew closer.

A few weeks ago things seemed to shift—although the change had been so subtle she'd worried she was imagining it. Coral noticed Sage was almost always at the diner when she came in for lunch. At first, she'd been hesitant to accept when he motioned her over to his table, after all, he was one of the largest ranchers in the state. Sage Morgan was well respected and from a good family.

Coral's own reputation was intact—mostly. The only

thing tainting it was her family. Well, her family and the fact she had a job that wasn't ever going to make her rich. She loved her employer, but the truth was there wasn't really any room for advancement. Without any sort of formal education, she was probably going to be stuck working as a sales clerk forever. Sighing to herself, Coral wondered how she had managed to get painted into what seemed like an ever-shrinking corner.

Before Sage started eating lunch at the diner, several other local men had seemed interested in her, but now they all walked a polite, but very wide circle around her. It wasn't as if Coral's lunches with Sage meant she was giving up a banging social life, but she had finally started making friends and had hoped to begin dating again. And even though she'd been fantasizing about Sage Morgan almost every night since she'd met him, he had never asked her out on a date—why she'd clung to the fantasy for so long she wasn't sure. Of course, Murphy's Law was always in full effect when it came to Coral, so the minute she decided to begin looking elsewhere for companionship—the calls started.

And now, after the third week of those *I-know-where-you-are* phone calls, she was probably going to have to move on again soon—and wasn't that a depressing thought. She needed to get a little bit more money put together so she'd actually be able to get all the way to Portland this time. She hated to leave, but she didn't want her boss getting caught in the crossfire either. Charlotte O'Donnell had treated her like a daughter, and it was going to break her heart to have to leave, but she wanted the older woman be safe—and *that* meant moving on. Coral felt her eyes fill with tears she didn't dare let fall. *Crying never fixed a damned thing, Coral Ann.*

"Good afternoon, Charlotte." Coral was brought back to the moment by Sage's deep voice as he greeted her boss. *For God's sake, why don't I just swoon and fall off the ladder? Yep, falling in a heap at his feet will prove why you're a bad bet as date material.*

Charlotte O'Donnell had given Coral a job and a place to live when she'd needed it the most, and the elderly woman was the closest thing to a mother Coral had ever known. Coral thought back the evening late last summer when her car had decided to tank outside downtown Pine Creek, Montana's only small diner. That mechanical mishap turned out to be the biggest blessing she'd ever received. Just like that, recalling the events that led her to that moment made Coral shudder. *Shit! Hold still you idiot, he's going to hear the damned ladder rattle and know you're up here.*

The conversation that had been taking place below her paused, and Coral held her breath. If it was possible for someone to *think* themselves invisible she would have vanished into thin air. *Just hold on for a few more seconds. He'll sign his ticket and move on.* Sage and his brothers were among Charlotte's most loyal customers. At least one of them was in every day, and usually Coral saw more than one of the Morgans at some point before the store closed. O'Donnell Hardware was a throwback to an earlier era when small mom and pop businesses lined the main streets of small towns. A time when everyone in town knew everyone else, and kids played outside until the streetlights came on and no one worried.

Coral hated the fact so many of those small businesses had closed their doors, but their inability to compete with superstores was making places like O'Donnell's few and far between. Coral knew Charlotte was trying to keep the store profitable until she finally decided to retire. The elderly woman probably could have retired a decade ago, but for a woman who had worked hard all her life, retirement was meant for those who *couldn't* work. And as long as she *could* work, she planned to. She'd told Coral several times retirement didn't have anything to do with age.

"What was that?" Sage's question cut through Coral's musings but not the black spots dancing in her vision. *Fuck a fat fairy. I have to stop holding my damned breath every time that hot cowboy walks into this store. He's going to think I'm a Froot Loop. Damn it, I'm going to end up with fricking brain damage from a lack of oxygen. Why doesn't he just go? How long can it take to buy rope anyway?* At least her subconscious mind had been paying attention. *That's awfully soft rope. Wonder what he plans to do with that?* Even the black dots didn't obscure the erotic picture that flashed through Coral's mind. *Leapin' lizards I really do have to stop reading all those erotic romances.*

The disaster that came next would have made Lucille Ball proud. Just as Coral realized her fingers were slowing slipping from the ancient wooden ladder's smooth top rung, Sage's commanding voice cut through the fog, "Coral? What the hell are you doing up there? Come down here before you…" was the last thing she heard before everything around her faded from her vision, and the world dropped out from under her. Those pesky black spots melted together blocking out every single defense she'd erected and Coral let herself fall into a sweet blissful void of nothingness.

SAGE HAD COME into the hardware store hoping to bump in

to the most interesting woman he'd ever met. Coral Williams had seemed intent on keeping him at arm's length ever since she'd arrived in town, but Sage had finally decided to step up his pursuit of the skittish little mare who had caught his eye. There was something about her that called to him, and he'd spent months trying to pinpoint what it was before finally admitting it was everything. She was the very definition of petite. Hell, if she was more than an inch or two over five feet he'd eat his Stetson. Slender, but with sweet curves in all the right places, he spent more time than he cared to admit wondering what she would look like out of those worn out Levis.

Coral's dark chestnut colored hair was streaked with gold highlights making him think it had been painted by the angels before they'd sent her into his path. Every person who'd been in the diner the day she arrived had told him the first thing they'd noticed was the way she almost seemed to glow as she stepped through the door. Hell, Sage had yet to meet a single person who didn't think Coral hung the moon and stars—and in Big Sky Country *that* was saying a lot.

He really needed to get this figured out—she was turning him into a sap. If he wasn't careful he was going to end up sounding like a fucking Hallmark card. And he really wanted his damned brothers off his case. Jesus, Joseph, and Mary they were teasing him relentlessly about the way he was "not-handling" the situation. They hadn't been impressed by his slow progress, citing his lunches with her as worthy of a junior high school crush rather than a man who had been trained as a Master for more years than he could remember. Evidently, all the training in the world as a sexual Dominant didn't matter a twit when you were hit by a bolt of pure lust-lightning.

Truth was, it had been his conversation with Sally over at the diner that had sealed his change of direction. When Sally had confided how awful she'd felt on Christmas Eve when she had finally had to shoo Coral out the door so she could close up the diner. Sally told him Coral had obviously been trying to stay away from her lonely apartment as long as possible, nursing a small cup of hot tea for more than an hour. Sally's soft blue eyes had filled with tears as she'd confided in him. "It broke my heart to send her home, Sage. I tried to get her to come home with me, but she didn't want to impose on my family's Christmas. Damn, I was almost sick by the time I got home for worrying about her."

The idea of the sweet woman he'd spent months coaxing closer like a timid colt spending Christmas alone sent a lance of pain straight through his own heart, as it had Sally's. Knowing she'd been alone while he and his brothers shared the holiday with a lively parade of family and friends moving in a steady stream through their enormous log home had solidified his determination, Sage would make sure she attended their annual New Year's celebration. *Damned stubborn woman isn't going to ring in the New Year alone—it's just that simple.*

The first time he'd laid eyes on Coral she'd been bent over the hardware bins trying to find some obscure, specialty nails old man Stevens had asked her for. Sage had known instantly the old fart didn't need the nails, but was using the request as an excuse to look at the pretty brunette's luscious ass. When Sage leveled a look at the old man with knowing suspicion, Stevens had become flustered, and assured the young woman he'd return later after she'd had time to look for the unusual piece of hardware.

When Coral stood up and turned his way, Sage felt all

the air leave his lungs in a crushing whoosh. Her long hair had fallen in a cascade of chestnut waves over her shoulders, framing her heart-shaped face as the sunlight caught the golden highlights. It made it look like light fairies were dancing around her. Damned if those rumors about *glowing* hadn't been exactly right. Her cheeks were a deep pink from leaning over and her chocolate brown eyes glittered with mischief. "Okay Mr. Stevens, I'll keep looking if you're sure they are down there. And I'll check with Charlotte when she gets back from the doctor's office too." Coral had spoken to Mr. Stevens, but she'd locked gazes with him.

Old man Stevens had nodded and then turned toward Sage and winked as he'd hobbled out of the small store. *Sly fox still knows how to corner his prey even if he's too old to chase it.* When he returned his attention to Charlotte's new clerk, she smiled, and his heart had nearly stopped. She'd swiped her dusty hands down the front of her faded jeans and then held out her small hand. "Hi, I'm Coral. It's nice to meet you. What can I help you find?" The instant their hands had touched heat sparked in every cell in his palm before racing up his arm, and spreading through the rest of his body in a searing arc heating every part of him at the speed of light. Sage had done his share of battles with electric fences over the years, but nothing had prepared him for the shock waves Coral's touch left in its wake.

Hell, Sage thought his brain must have been a bit fried, because it had taken him a few seconds to realize he hadn't answered her question, or released her hand. Reluctantly releasing his grip, he'd let her fingers linger over his as he withdrew slowly. "Hi, I'm Sage Morgan. My brothers and I own the 5M Ranch north of town. I'm sure you'll be meeting them all at some time or another. I'm here to pick up the fencing supplies Charlotte ordered in for us. She left me a message this morning saying everything was here."

"Well, it's nice to meet you Mr. Morgan and let's..." it was all she'd gotten out before Sage had interrupted her, because having Coral call him Mr. Morgan wasn't going to do at all.

"Please, call me Sage. Mr. Morgan is my pop, and you'll probably meet him soon enough since he and Mom are back for the summer. But watch out for him, because no man raises five sons without becoming a real character." Coral's enormous smile had been as bright as the morning sun, and just as welcome. Something about the pretty young woman standing in front of him warmed the ice he'd kept around his heart after his ex's betrayal, and knowing he'd been the one to send that sparkling smile dancing over her sweet face was an added bonus.

Fuck, just thinking about his ex-girlfriend made him feel like his blood pressure was spiking. Everything about Mackenzie Leigh had been an illusion, and remembering how she'd fooled him sent a wave of fury through Sage. How the hell had he not realized what a viper that woman was? She was wicked to the core. Sage wasn't sure he'd ever been so deluded by anyone. And the worst of it had been the fact Sage had nearly destroyed his relationship with Brandt before he'd come to his senses. He counted himself lucky since he'd had almost an entire year of peace and quiet—fuck it, a lifetime wouldn't be enough time between them in his opinion. But, evidently the rumor mill had started churning the minute he'd taken an interest in Coral, because messages from Mackenzie had begun within a few days of their first meeting. The past month he'd gotten texts almost daily.

Sage had wondered a thousand times why he'd made

an exception to his "no repeat dating" with the viperous bitch—his only explanation was the fact he'd only seen the carefully crafted side of her she'd wanted him to see. Where she'd gotten the crazy notion he'd consider reconciling with her after she'd almost managed to ruin both his and his brother's reputation was a mystery for the ages, but he'd given up trying to explain "crazy" a long time ago.

## Chapter Two

THINKING BACK ON the day they'd met, Sage remembered how Coral hadn't batted an eye about helping him transfer the large pallet of supplies onto the flatbed of his truck. She had somehow even managed to make sure everything stayed nicely sorted so it would be easier to unload once he returned home. It had been hard work, but she'd stuck it out until the job was completed. He'd been damned impressed, and told her so. Coral had tilted her head to the side as if trying to figure out whether or not he was being sarcastic before simply explaining it was what Charlotte had hired her to do.

They'd chatted for a few minutes before he'd driven back to the ranch lost in his thoughts about the woman he'd just met. Sage had been impressed with Coral's insightful questions about ranch life, and her cautious enthusiasm for her new hometown. A few of her questions had seemed oddly out of place, and he remembered wondering how she could seem so skittish and gregarious at the same time. He knew women didn't usually travel alone across the country without becoming a bit cautious, but she seemed oddly focused on whether or not the locals looked after one another? He'd briefly wondered who or what such a sweet woman could be hiding from, but he'd let it go.

Sage knew his immediate physical attraction had been

more than a little influential in the decision, but Coral Williams was the first woman he'd even given a second glance since exorcizing Mackenzie from his life, and he hadn't been willing to let go of the feeling his libido might not be dead after all. It wasn't as if he hadn't played at the club since he'd broken up with Mackenzie, but in Sage's opinion sex during play was nothing more than physical relief. The attraction he felt for Coral was something else entirely.

During their short chat, Coral had reluctantly admitted Charlotte had rented her the tiny apartment above the store—a place Sage had known Charlotte hadn't rented out to anyone in almost a decade. *Christ, what kind of condition had the place been in? Couldn't have been good, that's for sure.* He and his brothers were all pretty good handymen and carpenters. It had crossed his mind to check the stairs at the back of the store that led up to the apartment the next time he was in town. Winters in Montana were usually brutal and those old stairs had been through too many to count.

After meeting Coral for the first time, he'd updated his brothers on Charlotte's newest employee during one of the rare occasions all five Morgan brothers managed to sit together for an evening meal. When they'd all expressed interest, he'd had to bite his tongue to keep from staking a claim. Not surprisingly, it had been Kip who'd gone straight to the heart of the matter, "You going after her big brother? Because if not, I'm thinkin' maybe I ought to make a trip to hardware store real soon." Kip was the youngest and the most impulsive of the five of them, and he was also a first class horn dog who attracted women like a magnet. Even at the tender age of twenty-five he had already worked his way through most of the female population in a hundred mile radius.

"You might want to reconsider that decision little brother." Colt's words barely covered his chuckle. "I'd say the eat shit and die look you're getting' from Sage is mighty meaningful—if you catch my drift." Brandt and Phoenix both laughed as Sage picked up his plate, and moved to the sink to rinse the dish before placing it in the dishwasher. He had known his brothers were teasing but it hadn't stopped the spark of jealousy that had flared inside of him. Hell, he'd never been jealous of a woman before because he'd always made every effort to avoid entanglements whenever possible. *But you were never jealous of Mackenzie and God knows she pulled every trick in the book to make you that way. So what's so special about this woman?*

Over the past year, Sage hadn't dated the same woman more than a time or two. And even then, he'd made sure she understood the way things were from the beginning— he had no intention of making another disastrous decision. But even now, several months later, he still remembered the moment—standing at the sink in their kitchen and knowing to the depths of his soul there had been something very special about Coral. He hadn't been able to shut down the sense of possessiveness he's felt surge to the surface at Kip's taunt, and even though it wasn't a feeling he was particularly proud of, it had still been there.

SAGE HAD KNOWN Coral was nearby when he'd entered the store because he'd caught a whiff of the delicious fresh citrus scent that always seemed to surround her. *Christ, I'm going to start getting a fucking hard-on every morning when I drink orange juice if I'm not careful.* He'd wondered where she gotten off to when the ladder next to him had suddenly rattled. Sage looked up just in time to see her fingers slipping from the top rung, her eyes had already been closing, and the entire scene seemed to play out in slow motion. He'd easily caught her in his arms and been shocked at how slight she felt in his arms. *Christ, doesn't the woman eat anything at all? She can't weigh a hundred pounds.* He was overcome with an almost overwhelming urge to protect her, a feeling he'd barely been holding back for the past five months—but now it consumed him.

Charlotte was beside herself with worry and Sage had to smile at the elderly woman's mothering of Coral. When Charlotte's husband died several years ago, many in their small town had become convinced the feisty older woman was going to follow him to the grave. Charlotte had fallen into a depression so deep word of her struggles eventually made its way to Brandt, even though he'd been deployed on the other side of the globe at the time. Amazingly, the middle Morgan son had managed to convince his Commander he needed a short leave and Brandt had returned home to check on his former employer.

The summer before joining the Navy, Brandt had helped the O'Donnell's out at their store. Sage wasn't sure what had forged their bond, but Ben and Charlotte had both treated Brandt like a son as long as Sage could remember. He'd never known for sure how Brandt had gotten the short leave or what he'd said to Charlotte during the days he spent with her—but the difference in her had been noticeable. To this day the two of them were close, and now it looked as if Charlotte was becoming equally attached to Coral Williams.

Charlotte's battle back from her grief had been a long, slow process. But Brandt's visit had been the turning point, and the locals had been relieved to know she would eventually make her way back to them. Pine Creek was a small town, and the sense of community strong. There had been a collective sigh of relief when they'd started seeing glimpses of the old Charlotte reemerge. When Brandt returned home to stay he'd taken the part-time job as a deputy. Hell, the two of them still spent time together whenever they could. When the former sheriff died, Brandt inherited his position, and his time with Charlotte was often cut short. His younger brother was essentially the only law enforcement officer for miles around, leaving little time for anything personal. Sage had never heard Charlotte complain, but he'd seen the loneliness creeping back into her soft blue eyes. Coral's arrival had seemed to put the spring back in Charlotte's step, and everyone who knew her was thrilled with the change. "Oh my. Do you think we should call Doc? I have no idea what to do? She was fine before you came in. We were chatting up a storm. But she does seem to get mighty flustered anytime you're around."

The significance of Charlotte's words wasn't lost on Sage. *Could she be as attracted to me as I am to her? Fuck, maybe I've been wasting valuable time.* "Well, she was awfully quiet up there. I didn't even know she was there." *So I am wondering if she was even breathing.* He sat down on a pallet of feedbags, and settled her on his lap. When her eyes fluttered open, he grinned at her startled expression. "Surprised, sweet cheeks? I was too. It isn't every day the good Lord drops a gorgeous woman right into my arms. I think I'll buy a lottery ticket at the Stop 'n Go before I leave town, because I'm fairly certain this is my lucky day."

She was looking at him with eyes that were bedroom soft, and he could see she wasn't back to herself. Her eyes weren't focusing on anything. When he pressed his lips softly against her forehead she closed her eyes again, whispering, "Wow, what a great dream. No hot sex, but still awfully nice. Warm and snuggly too." When he looked up at Charlotte, she was grinning like the Cheshire Cat, and she quickly pressed her palm over her mouth before the laughter he saw in her eyes managed to escape. Yes, indeed, it seemed the sweet old woman had been keeping information from him—Sage would be having a chat with Charlotte about that one day soon.

When Charlotte nodded her head to the side letting him know she'd was heading back the front of the store he nodded and grinned. He could barely believe what he'd heard and he was planning to use is shamefully to his advantage. "Hey Sleeping Beauty time to rise and shine." He felt her go completely still in his arms a second before her eyes popped wide open, and she started frantically trying to scramble off his lap. "Oh no you don't, sweetness. You stay right where you are for a minute. I want to make sure you are alright before I let go of the most beautiful woman to ever fall into my arms."

She turned her face into his chest, but not before he saw her blush so deeply he could actually feel the warmth of her cheeks through his flannel shirt. "Oh my God, please, please, please tell me I didn't say all of that out loud. I swear I'll die of humiliation if I did."

"Well, since I was hoping you'd come to our New Year's celebration, I'm sure not going to say anything that might make you expire from humiliation. So how about this? I won't mention all the times I've dreamt about holding you like this, and you don't have to tell me about *your* dreams." *Yet.* "How does that sound?" She still had her face buried in his chest and when she nodded he couldn't hold back his laughter. "Sweetness, someday very soon nodding is not going to work for ya. You're going to have to answer questions with words. Now, up with you. And I'm not going to take no for an answer to my party invitation. Seems the least you could do, after all I caught you before you before you made your way all the way to the floor."

He set her on her feet, but kept his hands on her hips until she was steady. She was too thin, that was for sure, and he was sure she'd lost weight since she'd moved to town. Hell, now that he considered it, she'd lost quite a bit of weight in the past month. "Hand me your phone sweetness, and let me program in the directions to the ranch." When she seemed to hesitate he raised a brow and studied her. "Coral is there some reason I can't see your phone?" Her almost imperceptible tensing might have been missed by some men, but Sage had been a Dom too many years to miss even the slightest response. He may not get to the club down in Billings very often, but he damned sure hadn't slipped enough to miss her hesitance or the flash of fear that went across her pretty face.

When she pulled the phone from her pocket and started to activate it herself, he gently took it from her fingers and opened it. *Twenty missed calls? In the past two hours? And all of them from "Unavailable" according to her caller ID?* Sliding the small electronic device into his breast pocket, he watched her for several seconds before speaking. "I'll tell you what, since it's almost closing time, I'm going to tell Charlotte I'm kidnapping you to have dinner with me at the diner. You get your jacket and meet me by the front door in two minutes. And don't you even think about trying to ditch me, sweetness, or I'll add another punishment to your tab."

Her eyes went impossibly wide, and her voice was the perfect mixture of apprehension and anticipation that never failed to make him rock hard. "Another?"

"Another. I'm going to have to teach you how important it is to ask for help when you need it, sweetness. I'm not a fool, and I know full well these missed calls are a problem for you. I'm also betting they are at least part of the reason you've lost so much weight recently, and your pretty ivory skin has those dark circles under your eyes." He turned her toward the back of the store and gave her heart shaped ass a gentle swat, "Now go, your two minutes start *now*."

# Chapter Three

SAGE KEPT HIS palm pressed against Coral's lower back as they walked the half block to the diner, knowing it would set the tone for what was to come. *Begin as you intend to go.* The sexual Dominant inside Sage knew keeping Coral settled in his presence, and gaining her trust was going to be crucial to finding out what was going on. But the man inside was fighting a furious battle to keep from demanding answers. The same surge of possessiveness he'd felt at his brothers' taunts was back, and he was struggling to keep from throwing her over his shoulder and heading straight back to the ranch.

Once they'd settled into one of the back booths and placed their orders, he'd looked at her expectantly. When she didn't respond immediately, he leaned forward and grinned. "We can do this one of two ways, sweetness. I can interrogate you and pull the information out of you, or you can save us both a lot of time and frustration by just coming straight out with it. Tell me what's going on and how I can help."

He watched her closely and could almost hear the wheels spinning as she weighed her options. The small diner wasn't full yet, but the smell of dinners waiting to be served mingled with the scent of freshly baked bread and cinnamon rolls. When he heard her stomach growl, he smiled—at least she didn't seem to be in any hurry to rush back out the door. "How about I help you get started. Tell me why you haven't been eating. Money or stress?"

Instantly her eyes were swimming in unshed tears. "How did you know?" Her whispered question tore at his heart, because it was obvious she wasn't accustomed to anyone taking any personal interest in her. *That* was about to change in a very big way, but he didn't think she was quite ready to hear it yet. If he made Coral Williams his own, he'd know more about her sweet body than she did. There wouldn't be a square inch he didn't map with tender kisses and licks.

"Well darlin', I pay attention to details. Success is always in the details, and I've been interested in you since the first time I saw you. Now, answer the question." Sage made sure he put enough command in the last sentence she wouldn't mistake it as a request.

She immediately lowered her eyes to her clasped hands resting on the table. *Ahh, pretty girl my suspicions were right. Such a sweet little sub.* "Well both actually. The calls are…well they are worrisome." *Yeah, I fucking bet they are.* "I know I'm going to have to move on soon even though I don't really want to, so I'm trying to save money." She took a deep breath and let it out slowly before going on. "Sometimes, I just can't face eating another package of Ramen Noodles for dinner, you know? So I skip eating altogether." Her chuckle was hollow, and he knew how much effort it had taken her.

"Please don't tell Charlotte. She'd have a fit and I know she can't afford to pay me more. I've seen the daily sales numbers, and I honestly don't know how she can afford to pay me at all." Sage barely managed to hold back a howl of laughter at Coral's observation because Charlotte O'Donnell was probably one of the richest people in the state. Both she and her late husband had come from very wealthy families. Both families owned thousands of acres and the land was covering billions of dollars in natural gas that had only recently been tapped. Charlotte and Ben had never lived lavishly, and hadn't been blessed with children so their fortune had grown exponentially over the years. Sage didn't even want to attempt an estimate of what Charlotte's net worth might be.

Even though he knew it was absurd—he held up two fingers. "Scout's honor, I won't say a thing about your poor eating habits to Charlotte—on one condition." He gave her a second to process the fact he was going to expect something in return, before adding, "As long as you agree to eat with me whenever I ask you to." She might have been eating at the diner, but he'd noticed most days she'd simply ordered a small cup of soup. Some might have seen his "bargain" as blackmail, or was it extortion? Hell, he'd never been able to remember which was which—that was Brandt's area of expertise, not his. Sage had a sinking feeling they were going to be needing Brandt for more than a couple of legal definitions in the very near future.

While they ate their hot beef sandwiches, Coral slowly told him her story. Every new detail gave him added respect for the brave woman sitting across from him. "My parents were killed by a teen driver who was texting. The little twerp wasn't even charged because his parents owned the local bank and...well, my mom and dad weren't exactly pillars of the community." Covering her hand with his own, he gave her an encouraging squeeze. She took a deep breath before continuing, "I was paralyzed by grief. I didn't have any other family and even though I didn't approve of everything my mom and dad did—well, they were all I had. And then all of the sudden they were gone. I barely scraped together enough money to bury them, and paying off their mortgage? Forget about that. The bank president whose son who was driving the car the broadsided mom and dad was all too happy to send me an eviction notice."

Sage made a silent vow to destroy the man who'd wanted his son's crime pushed into the past badly enough to essentially kick Coral out of her own home. "I'd been living at home to save money while I took a couple of classes at the local junior college. But when I had to move, I had to quit and start working full-time." He saw the wistfulness in her eyes and hated the fact her life had been so difficult. "As you can imagine, the employment opportunities in rural Georgia are pretty slim when you don't have an education, so I packed up everything that would fit in my car and moved in with the guy I'd been dating. He lived closer to Atlanta, and I'd hoped I could find a good job there."

"It didn't take me long to know I'd made a huge mistake moving in with him. We hadn't been dating for long and ordinarily I wouldn't have even considered it, but..." Sage didn't say anything as she let the sentence trail off into a long pause. Obviously she hadn't seen any other options, and his chest tightened when he thought about how close she'd come to being homeless.

Coral took a deep breath and continued, "I'd evidently had my head in the sand because I usually have better instincts. But after a few days watching the constant flow of people in and out of the apartment, the hushed conversations, and flashes of money changing hands I knew exactly what I'd gotten myself into. I didn't say anything to him, I just moved a few of my things out into the trunk of my car each day until there was nothing left in the house. I'd planned to leave on Friday morning, because he'd said he was driving to Atlanta for the weekend. I thought it would give me a few days head start. He gotten really hateful since I'd moved in and more than a little paranoid."

Sage watched as she stirred her potatoes around aimlessly on her plate for several seconds. He'd almost decided he was going to have to start asking questions when she looked up at him. Sage knew he'd never forget the haunted look in her beautiful eyes as she spoke, "I thought he'd already left…I really did. I'd heard the front door slam, so I grabbed my purse and keys and started down the hall toward the living room. I heard a loud pop—like a balloon and I looked up in time to see the man I'd been dating tucking the pistol into the back of his pants and two of his buddies grabbing a guy on the floor by the ankles."

She took a deep breath, and then blew it out slowly before continuing. "I ducked into the bathroom and shut the door before they saw me. But the window was so high and so small I had a hard time fitting through it. I was finally squeezing past the frame, when change fell out of my jacket pocket and hit the floor of the bathroom. My boyfriend was immediately pounding on the door yelling at me to come out. I dropped from the second story window onto the ground. I was lucky, the ground was really soft from the rain we'd had overnight otherwise I'm probably would have broken my ankles."

Sage was seething with anger Coral had been in so much danger, the fury roiling inside him threatening to burst at any second. He let his gaze flicker to the tumbler of water sitting in front of him. Damn it would make a satisfying crunch as it hit the wall at the other side of the room. The temptation was almost too much to resist because he was certain he'd feel at least marginally better for a few breaths. But as a Dom, Sage knew the quickest way to shut down a submissive was to react emotionally to their story—particularly if the emotion was negative. A sub's innate desire to please meant they often withheld information simply to avoid negative reactions from those around them, and it didn't matter if the reaction wasn't directed at them—the reaction was the same.

"I ran behind the neighbor's fence, and then made my way through the parking lot. I had a small pocketknife in my purse, so I flattened as many tires as I could on cars I knew were theirs before running to my own car. I always had to park down the street so his *friends* could part close. In hindsight, I think I should be more grateful for that, huh?" Coral's eyes were swimming in unshed tears. Her sad attempt at humor hadn't done anything for Sage or for her.

Sage felt like his heart was being ripped from his chest as she talked about how she'd driven for days without sleep. "It wasn't so bad actually, because every time I fell asleep I kept seeing *that* gun...and the man on the floor. So I wasn't really getting any sleep anyway." She shuddered, her eyes closed against a horror Sage knew she'd probably be haunted by for years to come.

"I've continued to checked newspapers when I can. I've only seen one brief mention about a missing drug dealer, but there wasn't much information in the short article. Since I have to drive to larger towns to get internet access, I don't get to check often now. Honestly, I'm afraid to check too often. I ditched my phone pretty quickly because I was afraid he'd find a way to track it. I used disposable phones until about three months ago. I finally got a real phone because it was so hard to remember to buy minutes. I was afraid to go without a phone, you know? I don't know how he got the number. I haven't given it to anyone but Charlotte." Her voice had finally faded to a whisper. The tears filling her eyes were close to falling, and Sage wanted nothing more than to pull her into his arms and never let her go. It was time to get her out of the small diner, she had already had enough of her dignity stolen—he wasn't going to compound the problem by putting her emotions on public display.

"Sweetness, if you are finished eating, I'd like to get out of here. We need to figure out exactly how we're going to keep you safe. And quite frankly, I need to just hold you for a minute." He'd kept his voice level—a miracle considering the fury pulsing through his system. He was going to have to call Brandt in and he wasn't sure how Coral was going to handle it. Additionally, he didn't want to risk her reputation by having what would likely be a strained conversation with the local sheriff in a public place.

He saw her take a fortifying breath, and knew she was working on every possible excuse to keep him from helping her. *Good luck with that, sweetheart. Not gonna happen.* As soon as they were on the sidewalk he turned her, pulling her into his embrace. God, she was so small against him. Her cheek rested against his heart. He held her close until he felt her relax into his hold. Inhaling the frigid air, he pulled back enough to look down into her dark eyes. "Coral, the first thing I'm going to say is you are no longer facing any of this alone. Remember that, sweetness, because it's important. And I know you are worrying about involving anyone else." When her eyes widened in surprise, he laughed. "Pet, it's written all over your face. Now, Charlotte told me you have tomorrow off, so let's go up to your apartment. I want you to pack up a few things, and I'm taking you out to the ranch." When she started to protest he held up his hand to stop her. "Coral, do you trust me? Have I or any of my brothers ever given you any cause to be afraid of us? Hell, Brandt is the damned Sheriff. Do you think he'd let us hurt or take advantage of you?"

He saw her shoulders relax as she considered his words. Sage chuckled, hoping his smile would put an end to her doubt. "Jesus, Joseph, and Mary, the whole lot of us are more afraid of Charlotte and our own pop than we are of most anything else you could imagine. And I assure you, if either of them found out we had treated you like anything but a princess, there would be hell to pay for sure."

As they rounded the corner he heard the door of her little apartment close. Sage quickly pulled her behind him, and stepped into the shadows. Sage and Coral stood stone still listening, as the two men descending the stairs at the back of O'Donnell Hardware cursed the fact their target hadn't been home. Evidently kidnappers didn't relish the thought of having to make more than one attempt to capture their quarry. Sage shook his head in disbelief. *What the hell kind of two-bit hoods are these guys anyway?*

As the two men got into a dark sedan, Sage was betting was a rental, he heard one of them say something about "the bitch being positive the girl would be there by now" but he hadn't been able to hear the partner's response. Sage wondered if Coral had been completely upfront with him or if perhaps her *boyfriend* had been seeing someone else on the side.

After they'd driven away, Coral shifted so she could step around him, but Sage stilled her. Leaning down, he brushed the silken curls that had escaped her ponytail aside, to speak against her ear. "Sweetness, this could be a trap. Is there anything up there you can't live without tonight?" When she shook her head, he kissed the shell of her ear and wanted to smile at the shiver he felt move through her.

*Obviously the lady is at least attracted to me—it's a start.* "Alright then, let's get out of here."

He'd parked in the alley a couple of doors down from the hardware store. Keeping them in the shadows, Sage moved quickly to the passenger's side of his truck. Lifting her easily into the cab, he leaned across her to secure her seatbelt and noticed she was crying. "Oh baby, please don't cry—you're breaking my heart. I promise we'll keep you safe."

"I'm sorry. I hate to cry, but I'm so tired of being scared. It's exhausting. I had finally gotten to the place where I could sleep all night again. And now…well, now it's all starting over. I thought I'd escaped. I went clear across the country. Why won't they just let me go? Obviously I'm not going to tell anyone after all this time." Sage knew exactly why they were tracking her, and he was pretty sure she did too. There was no way her ex was going to leave such a large loose end. An eyewitness to a murder would be definitely be an enormous problem, but there really wasn't anything to be gained by saying *that* out loud.

He'd placed his hands on both sides of her face, and used his thumbs to gently brush away her tears. He kissed the end of her nose and smiled. "Let's get you home, sweetness." It wasn't until he was buckled in and was driving he realized the significance of the words he'd spoken to Coral. But rather than them sounding odd, somehow they'd sounded exactly right.

## Chapter Four

USING THE HANDS free device in his truck, Sage called Brandt letting him know there had been a break-in at Coral's apartment, and briefly explaining what they'd seen and heard. "Coral is with me, I'm taking her home with me." *And I intend to keep her there.* "Give me a call when you can." Sage knew Brandt would understand his statement translated to, I want to talk to you when Coral can't hear our conversation.

Brandt's voice boomed through the truck's speakers, "I'm heading that way now. I wasn't in town, so it's going to take me a few minutes to get there. Is there anything Coral would like me to bring from her apartment when I come home?" She nodded and rattled off a short list, including a backpack she said contained a change of clothes, a small makeup bag, hairbrush, her e-reader, and a teddy bear. Brandt chuckled, but Sage heard the underlying tension in his brother's voice as he assured her he'd strap the bear in carefully before heading out to the ranch. Sage wasn't sure which of the things Coral asked for Brandt had taken issue with, but he intended to find out.

Sage was grateful Brandt had been gentle with Coral despite the thread of steel he'd heard in his brother's tone. The middle Morgan brother was probably the most hardline of any of them, and that attitude certainly wasn't what Coral needed tonight. Brandt's years as a Navy SEAL had hardened him in many ways and nothing seemed to be sanding down those sharp edges.

Sage hoped Brandt and his other brothers all found their women someday soon because the five of them had always planned to marry and raise their families together. None of them were getting any younger, something his mother had reminded him of just this morning. They had already completed three homes on the ranch and the other ones were started. Sage had always known he'd live in the main house, but there would be a lot of work to do before all the others had moved out.

As he pulled in front of the main house the one of the two large wooden doors opened before he'd even taken his truck out of gear. Colt, Phoenix and Kip all walked down the steps to greet them. Brandt had obviously given them a heads up. When he turned to tell Coral to wait for him to come around and help her, he saw she'd fallen asleep. Stepping from the truck, he turned to his brothers. "She's exhausted. Let me get her settled on the sofa in the living room, and then we'll talk in the kitchen. I doubt she sleeps long, but I want her to get any rest she can."

Sliding his arms under her, Sage lifted her into his arms. She settled against him perfectly, her soft breath wafting gently against the side of his neck, and sending a very strong message to his cock. *Goddamn it to hell. Walking with a hard-on is a pain in the ass.* Sage didn't waste any time getting her settled, covering her with a soft quilt his mom had given him a few months earlier. She'd told him she'd made it so he'd have something special to wrap his true love in when she finally made her way into his life. *I swear the woman is downright spooky sometimes.* His dad had often warned all five of his sons their mama's intuition was nothing to scoff at. And over the years they'd learned to listen to her, even when she didn't think they were.

The fireplace was already blazing, the room comfortably warm as the golden glow highlighted all the different shades of gold and auburn in her dark hair. Sage pressed a soft kiss to the top of her head before motioning his brothers out of the room. The deep purple half-moons under her eyes spoke volumes about everything she'd been dealing with, and he hoped like hell she'd be able to rest better under their roof. When he started to step away Phoenix shook his head and pointed at her threadbare canvas shoes.

Sage smiled, leave it to Phoenix to notice—he was the caretaker among them. Phoenix was the quietest and most sensitive of the five Morgan brothers. He was also absolutely brilliant. The computer games Phoenix Morgan created were among the most popular in the world. He'd also created several software programs that eased the ranch's endless bookkeeping in ways Sage would have never been able to imagine possible.

Phoenix's sensitive nature made him a natural with animals of all kinds, and the ranch hands often begged him for his help when they were trying to break a particularly skittish mare. Sage had never seen him fail with an animal, and much to his brother's chagrin, Phoenix didn't seem particularly interested in practicing those skills on a woman. Phoenix had always been painfully shy, and Sage had been surprised to see him chatting easily with Coral one day inside the hardware store. When he'd asked his brother about it later, he'd shrugged his shoulders and simply said she was easy to talk to.

Sitting down around their large kitchen table, Sage gave them an abbreviated update because he knew they were going to have to hear it all again as soon as Brandt made his way home. Colt's eyes were bright with fury. "So you're planning to keep her here, right? No way does she need to be in that apartment alone. Hell, you saw what those stairs were like when we worked on them last summer. I can't imagine the door is any more secure, I'd be surprised if it even locks."

Colt had helped Sage repair the stairs one evening last summer after they'd overheard Coral tell Charlotte she was planning to fix it herself. But since Coral hadn't been home at the time, they hadn't been able to check anything else in the small apartment. Now he knew she'd been driving to other towns to use the internet he understood her frequent unexplained absences.

"I want her to stay here. She will be safe here and—well, I want her close. Fuck me. I just *want* her period. She's smart, obviously resourceful, and brave—not to mention witty and kind. And the fact she is gorgeous is icing on a perfect piece of sweet cake." When Sage looked up, he knew by the grins on his brother's faces Coral must be standing behind him. He turned in his seat and his breath caught in his throat. Her tiny feet were now bare and her hair was a riot of chestnut waves that caught the light making it look as if light sprites were dancing in and out of her curls.

She must have gotten too warm and taken off the soft sweatshirt she'd been wearing because she was standing there in a tiny white T-shirt that didn't meet the top of her low cut jeans. He caught a glint off a gold ring in her navel and couldn't hold back his whispered, "Sweet Jesus, you are so fucking beautiful." She had already been blushing but at his words her cheeks were now nearly glowing. When he held his hand out to her, she walked straight to him with no hesitation, and he was lost to her in that moment. The brief show of trust was all it took to completely ensnare his heart. She was so petite he still had to look down into her eyes despite the fact he'd settled her on his lap. "Are you alright, sweetness?"

She nodded and leaned into him pressing her cheek against the front of his shoulder. He looked up at his brothers and saw affection in their eyes. When he first expressed an interest in Charlotte's new girl, each of his brothers had made a point to stop by the hardware store to meet her and introduce themselves. Sage was grateful now they'd each taken the time to get to know her. She was much more at ease now because of their efforts. He knew it would be far easier for Coral to be in a roomful of men she considered friends rather than those she merely considered acquaintances. Naturally it was Phoenix who leaned close and asked, "Coral, honey would you like something to drink? We probably have just about everything since we're ready for our New Year's Eve party."

She sat bolt upright, her eyes going wide as she looked at Sage. "Oh my stars. I forgot you mentioned a party. I didn't ask Brandt to bring me anything to wear that will be suitable for a party. How on earth am I going to help serve without something appropriate to wear? Oh frack, I can't believe I did this. Sometimes I'm pretty sure not all of my wiring is plugged in." *Serving? Did she just say serving? Oh, not on your life sweet girl.*

He placed his fingers under her chin making sure her focus remained on him. "Serving? You think I invited you here to *work*? Seriously?" Her eyes dilated and he heard her quick intake of breath—such a beautiful submissive response. He wanted to scoop her up and head right up to his bedroom—he'd show her exactly why he had invited her. He'd been planning to put her in the guest room but her reaction had sealed another fate for the two of them tonight. She would be sleeping in his bed rather than alone.

"No pet, you are not serving at the party. If you want to help out here and there we'll appreciate it, just as we would the help from any guest or family member." He'd deliberately changed his term of endearment, using one closely associated with D/s relationships. With his fingers wrapped around the back of her neck, he felt her pulse kick up at the reference. *Interesting.* "Now, Phoenix is awaiting your answer about a drink. I suggest you take him up on his offer because I just heard Brandt pull up and it's a safe bet he's going to have a lot of questions for you.

CORAL KNEW SHE'D surprised Sage when she leaned forward kissing him on the cheek before following Phoenix into the kitchen. The flair of desire in his eyes made her glad she'd taken the chance. As she walked out of the room she tried to finger comb her wild curls not realizing the motion would raise the hem her shirt enough to give the men behind her a nice view of the small scrollwork tattoo she had gotten as a teen. The soft colors swirled down and around the dimples at the top of her ass, though they couldn't have seen much of the intricate design. Hearing Sage's low growl gave her a thrill of satisfaction knowing she'd been able to affect him in some small way. Okay…if she was being honest, Coral should probably admit she was mentally bouncing up and down with smug self-satisfaction. Being able to affect the sexiest man she'd ever known by doing nothing more than sauntering out of the room, and flashing a bit of skin his way made her feel like a sex kitten—and it had been a really long time since she'd felt anything close to attractive.

Sage Morgan was the embodiment of everything Coral found sexy. His dark eyes truly were the windows to his soul. During the time she'd known him, Coral had learned to tell when he was teasing her by the way his eyes danced with mischief. She'd seen glimpses of his desire, but there had never been any promise he'd follow through...until tonight. That promise had shown itself briefly outside the diner earlier this evening, and listening to him talk about her with his brothers had given her another spark of hope. But the white-hot flash of desire she'd seen in his eyes when she'd pressed her lips against his tan cheek was a panty-soaking moment.

She helped Phoenix set drinks and a few snacks on trays, enjoying how easy Sage's younger brother was to work with. Coral tried not to stare at her surroundings with her chin dropped to her chest, and her mouth gaping open like a fish—but holy fricking crap on a pink cactus. Their kitchen would make any woman drool. It was huge. Phoenix laughed softly when he saw her taking it all in with wide eyes. "Remember, this is the main house and our mom raised five sons here—she also loves to entertain. Even now, when they are home for the summer or holidays, she does the majority of their entertaining here rather than at their smaller place in town. If you want to know the truth, I think we'll be building another house out back when grandkids come along. Neither Mom, nor Pop will want to live in town and miss a moment they could share with *their rewards for not stringing us up*—Pop's words, not mine by the way."

He laughed again when she cocked her head to the side in confusion. Grabbing her hand he led her toward one of several sets of French doors at the back of the room.

Pulling open a door just far enough for her to see outside, he pointed out the other houses setting around the perimeter of what appeared to be a long, oval beautifully landscaped yard. He told her which were finished and those they were still working on. He grinned as he drew her attention to the different features of the common area in the middle.

She was awestruck, but when she started to step outside to get a closer look, a strong arm wrapped around her waist pulling her back against rock hard abs. She knew without turning it was Sage who held her close—the scent he wore always made her pulse speed up and her girly parts take notice. "Where do you think you are going, pet? It's winter in Montana, baby. You don't go outside without a coat and shoes unless you're courting pneumonia." He leaned down and whispered against her ear, "And I have plans for you later that do not include you being ill." She heard Phoenix's snort of laughter behind them before Sage turned her back into the room. "Come." He held his hand out to her, nodding when she placed her small hand in his much larger one, before leading her back to the large table where everyone sat waiting.

When she looked up to see Brandt Morgan standing with his arms crossed over his massive chest and she instinctively took a step back. *Holy crap. He is freaking huge. And he looks pissed. He's a cop and I fled the scene of a crime. Of course he's pissed. Shit! What if he makes me go back there?* The terror she was feeling must have shown on her face because she saw Colt punch Brandt's shoulder. "Knock it off SEAL-boy you're scaring the shit out of her."

Coral didn't know Colt Morgan well, but she'd certainly heard a lot about his years on the rodeo circuit. Apparently he'd been some sort of bull riding superstar before being injured a couple of years ago at the National Finals. She'd also heard he had the voice of an angel if you could persuade him to sing for you—something that apparently only happened a few times a year at the local bar and grill…if you could believe the local rumor mill.

The tall, dark, and intimidating Sheriff dropped his arms, but his expression didn't soften, making him look every bit the authority figure he was. She'd never seen this formidable version of Brandt Morgan, and she briefly wondered if she wouldn't be better taking her chances with pneumonia by sprinting out the backdoor barefoot. The Sheriff nodded to a nearby chair, "Have a seat Coral, I have some questions for you." Suddenly she wanted to be anywhere but here. Her feet were in agreement with her mind's desire to flee because she took another step back coming up against Sage's rock hard chest once again.

"It's okay, sweetness. Don't mind his attitude. Brandt slips into badass Navy SEAL mode pretty easily—even when he *shouldn't*. We're hoping he manages to become more human when he finally grows up." Sage's comments brought chuckles from his brothers, but did little to reassure her. The man was radiating frustration and it all seemed to be focused on her.

Coral hadn't spent much time talking with Brandt despite the fact he came in to the hardware store regularly. He'd been polite, but she'd felt his reserve even as he'd been joking with Charlotte. When Coral commented on the difference she sensed in this Morgan brother, her boss had reminded her, "War changes people in ways you can't imagine, Coral. Brandt has seen the worst of humanity and it's going to take him a while to remember there is more *good* in the world than bad."

Coral spent the next two hours being grilled—there

wasn't any other way to describe the intense questioning she endured under Sheriff Brandt Morgan's glare. This man wasn't the easy-going—though distant, rural Sheriff—she'd met at the hardware store. No, this man was a formidable enemy and she suspected even as an ally he'd be a tough sell if you displayed even a hint of weakness. Coral was astute enough to know the man was frustrated beyond belief she hadn't come to him as soon as she'd started getting the phone calls. But, what he didn't seem to understand was how long she'd been on her own, and how few people she'd actually been able to trust.

She'd answered each of his questions with complete honesty even when it had broken her heart to reveal the many mistakes she'd made. Even though the men sitting around the table hadn't appeared to judge her, knowing they were listening had been humiliating enough. Sighing, she reminded herself it wouldn't do her any good to add lying to her already lengthy list of missteps, and in the end, who wanted friends who were unable to accept you the way you really were? Coral knew she was going to have to move on anyway, so it probably shouldn't matter...but it did. Knowing she wasn't going to be able to stay in Pine Creek depressed Coral far more than she would ever thought possible when she'd first found herself stranded in the small mountain town.

Sage reached over the table and took her hand in his and drawing her attention. "What were you thinking about just now that made you so sad, pet?" His question was quietly spoken but would certainly would have been heard by anyone paying attention. It touched her knowing he hadn't minded asking about her feelings in front of his brothers.

"I was thinking about how much I'm going to hate

leaving Pine Creek." She took a steadying breath before continuing, "Charlotte has been so good to me. And, I like the people here. Everyone has been so nice—well everyone but the one woman who comes in the store occasionally." In her peripheral vision, Coral saw Brandt's frown at the mention of a woman being rude, but he didn't press the issue.

When Coral asked Charlotte about the stunning blonde who'd stopped in a few times over the past few months, her boss had waved off her inquiry. "Don't you worry about her, that sack of trash has already been set on the curb." Coral had asked if the woman lived nearby, but Charlotte had simply said she wasn't worth worrying about.

Coral was absently rotating the bottom of her soda bottle making circles on the table as she thought back over the past year. *Frack, I'm going to miss this place.* Without looking up she finally added, "Although, it *is* outrageously cold in the winter." She laughed softly but even to her own ears the levity sounded forced. When she looked up, no one else was smiling. *They are probably thinking it wouldn't seem so damned cold if you'd spend the money to buy a good coat, Coral Anne. And I'll bet they think boots would be a damned good idea, too.* Her well-worn canvas shoes didn't do much to keep her feet dry in the snow. More than one of the store's customers had mentioned her lack of appropriate clothing. Hell, two of the men sitting across from her had reminded her to get a pair of boots before the first snowstorm of the season.

"Sweetness, we'll be having a long chat about your plans to leave *and* your deplorable lack of winter clothing—later—in private." *Holy crapamolie. Does he read minds or something? Because I'm pretty sure that would be damned unhandy at times.*

## Chapter Five

CORAL'S ENTIRE BODY was tingling and she knew it wasn't from the hot water raining down on her. The water jets were pummeling her tired muscles from various places where they were mounted along the walls of the biggest shower she'd ever seen. God in heaven it felt good to take a *hot* shower. Coral hadn't told Charlotte the hot water heater in her apartment wasn't working properly because she'd worried her sweet boss would spend money she couldn't afford to replace the antique fixture. Charlotte wasn't even charging her rent for goodness sake, how could she expect the woman to spend money updating a place that wasn't generating any income?

No, it wasn't the sinful shower making her body feel like it was buzzing in anticipation, what she was feeling now was pure anticipation. Sage hadn't made any secret of the fact he wanted her...she'd heard it downstairs when she first walked into their kitchen and overheard his conversation with his brothers. All these months she'd been fantasizing about him and now it seemed he'd been interested in her as well. Damn, that had been a pleasant surprise—but it was also a major complication. She didn't want to involve him or his family in her troubles—what if one of them was hurt because of her? They'd insist on protecting her and would become a target as well. Just thinking about *that* possibility made her almost physically ill.

When she'd first stepped into the open doorway of their enormous eat-in kitchen and heard him talking about her, Coral noticed each of the brothers sitting around the table shift subtly in their seats. Their expressions softened, but something in their eyes held her in place until he'd finished. The fact he had listed physical appearance last warmed her heart, knowing he appreciated attributes that wouldn't fade over time made her want him all the more. But Coral knew she needed to keep reminding herself, just because he wanted her now didn't mean there would be anything for the two of them long-term. *Guys like Sage Morgan don't marry girls from the other side of the tracks...don't forget that, Coral Anne.*

She gave herself a good talking to, listing off all the reasons a gorgeous, sexy, successful man would never be interested in keeping her. *I really do have to cut back on the romance novels.* The hot titles on her Kindle were her one indulgence and God only knew how many times she'd re-read her favorite series. "But men aren't really like that. Real men don't put a woman's pleasure first. It doesn't matter that Sage makes everything inside me desperate to feel him slide his cock so deep into my pussy he can feel my heart beat. I wonder if orgasms are real. And if they are, how do you know if you have one? Maybe it's all hype. Well, no matter. I have to remember the happily ever after is for the women on my e-reader, not for me. Damn it all to hailstones now I'm talking to myself...if the Morgan brothers heard this they'd already be making calls and ordering my cracker factory pass."

Leaning her head back so the water was massaging her scalp, she felt a hand wrap around her hair and she let out a yelp of surprise. Sage pulled her back until the only thing keeping her upright was his very wet and deliciously naked chest pressing against her back. "Cracker factory? Tell me sweetness, what is that exactly?" His actions might have been all about dominance and power, but his voice gave away his amusement.

"Didn't your mama ever teach you it's not nice to listen to crazy people talking to themselves? I'm pretty sure it falls under some sort of privacy and confidentiality clause. There has to be some rule about it *somewhere*." She was practically panting her words by the time she'd finished speaking. The man's touch was splintering her thoughts. Coral was actually damned impressed she'd been able to speak at all.

His free hand rubbed over her breasts, gently rolling her nipples into tight peaks, and the moisture coating her sex was already threatening to snake its way down the insides of her thighs. Yes, indeed…being able to put words together had been a noteworthy accomplishment for sure.

"OH, BABY, ONE of the things you need to learn right quick is how little influence my sweet mama's lessons have the instant that luscious ass of yours crosses the threshold into the master suite." Sage knew she was aroused, he could smell the sweet honey of her desire—the scent went straight to his cock, fueling an already raging hard-on. Sliding his fingers down her torso and through her slick folds, he smiled. "You are so wet baby. And I can't begin to tell you how much that pleases me. And yes, sweet girl, I believe you are going to find that orgasms live up to all the hype." Coral moaned as he circled her clit with his finger. He wasn't giving her the direct contact she needed to come, her hips were starting to rotate in nature's ancient dance of pleasure. "Are you on birth control?"

His question hadn't seemed to surprise her, but she seemed to be having trouble focusing long enough to answer, too. *Good, because she's doing a damned fine job of scrambling my brain cells, and I'd hate to go down alone.* He let the calloused pads of his fingers coax her clit out of hiding, giving her enough to keep her on edge, but not enough to send her over the edge. *Close...but not quite enough.* He doubted her mind fully understand what she was seeking, but her body had definitely gotten the memo. He wondered if she was going to answer the question, when she'd finally spoken. "Birth control...oh, yes. And, well, I haven't had much experience. Umm...he used condoms both times. Oh...damn that feels so good and I can't think when you... Oh..."

"What else were you going to say, baby?" When she started swaying to music only she could hear, Sage found himself completely enthralled with the sensuous woman in his arms. *Christ, she is the most responsive woman I've ever seen. Mine!* The surge of possessiveness surprised him, but he wasn't naïve enough to deny it. "It's going to only get more difficult to focus, sweetness. Best get your answer out now before you earn yourself another punishment. You've already got one coming you know, and I'm contemplating exactly what form it should take, so you might want to be particularly cooperative. You are, after all, naked and I've already made sure you'll stay well within my reach." He tightened his hold in her hair to emphasize the point before leaning down to bite gently on the top of her shoulder. That small bit of bondage elicited a low moan from Coral's plump lips as her knees folded out from under her. He chuckled. "Oh no, you don't get to come yet. Now, finish what you were saying before I'm forced to find another way to get your attention."

"I went to clinics…even with the condoms, I was scared. I went to a clinic in Billings and…well, I drove to Cheyenne too. I wanted to make sure he didn't give me anything. I'm clean…oh please don't stop." Her voice was taking on an air of desperation he always loved hearing when he played with subs. But it was different with Coral—this woman mattered more than any of the others had in the past. He wasn't going to demand she wait for permission to come, she obviously didn't have enough experience to delay an orgasm if she'd never had one. Hell, he doubted she'd be recognize the signs her release was coming until it steamrolled her. *That dry spell is fixin' to end right quick, baby.*

"Birth control, Coral?" She still hadn't answered his question, but he wasn't sure he wanted to know the answer either. For just a second a vision of her standing on the back terrace, her belly swollen with his child flashed through his mind, but he shoved it aside refocusing all of his attention on the beautiful woman in his arms.

"Yes, but…need…" Sage wanted to groan as her body shuddered against his. Damn, she was so fucking responsive he wasn't sure which one of them he was torturing more by withholding her pleasure. "Need to go again next…soon." *Aha that's what she's struggling to get out. That's an appointment she won't be going to alone, that's for sure.* After what he'd seen earlier outside her apartment, he didn't want her going anywhere alone—hell, if he had his way, he'd keep her sheltered at the ranch until everything was resolved.

He lifted her left leg, placing her foot on the stone bench built into the back wall of the large shower. The entire space was a hedonist's dream and for the first time since Sage remodeled the master en suite bathroom, he didn't feel even the slightest twinge of guilt about the obscene amount of money he'd spent on the small space. After his parents moved out, this had been the first renovation Sage had undertaken. He'd gutted the existing bathroom *and* the adjoining bedroom. He combined the two spaces into a bath suite that would make Architectural Digest sit up and take notice. The only argument his brothers had given him about the project was the size of the hot tub he'd chosen. He was glad he hadn't chosen an enormous hot tub because he wasn't interested in sharing with it anyone but the woman in his arms. And he was damned thrilled they'd recently completed the project. The tub might not be huge, but it was surrounded by soft lighting and rock shelves holding small pots of vining plants and white votive candles. The hidden speakers wrapped bathers in soothing sounds of the ocean or his personal favorite, the sound of falling rain and distant rumblings of thunder. Phoenix had also included several playlists of all Sage's favorite music into the system, and if the younger Morgan was true to form, he'd probably already found out Coral's favorites and added those as well.

The hot tub was nice, but the shower was his pride and joy. It was extra-large and featured numerous showerheads at various heights in addition to the two rain showerheads in the ceiling. There was a stone bench along the entire length of one wall. The bench was divided into sections of varying heights because he loved watersports of all kinds. The waterfall cascading down the rock wall was highlighted by backlights that made the water sparkle as it fell. The entire unit used recycled water removing any guilt over the amount of time he planned to spend enjoying his own personal water park. Montana winters were damned long, and he'd always dreamed of finding a woman who would love playing naked in the water as much as he did. Coral was lighting up under his touch. Hell, she was fucking perfect and didn't seem at all intimidated by the water pouring down around her.

With her pussy spread open to his touch, Sage began a full on assault of temptation with his fingers. She was already so close he didn't want to break the rhythm a second time by moving in front of her. "You are so perfect, baby. Your body melts against mine, your heartbeat has even synched to mine." Increasing the pressure against her clit, he smiled when she moaned softy. "You were made for me, sweetness. Let your body's desire lead you. Relax into my touch. Let go—let me take you there."

Coral's entire body was vibrating with need, and he knew she was fighting the unfamiliar sensations simply because they were overwhelming her. "It's mine, baby. Your pleasure belongs to me. Give it to me. *Now*." At his command Coral shattered in his arms. Her shout was almost completely silent, as if she hadn't had enough air to spare for the task. She shuddered with the convulsions of a release that had been almost violent—and it had been spectacular to watch. He was sure she hadn't noticed how she was fully displayed in the mirror at the end of the shower. Damn, he was glad he'd added the feature, because watching Coral come had been one of the hottest things he'd ever seen.

Her entire body had flushed a beautiful deep rose, and her scream had only been silent for a few seconds before the sound of her gasping his name echoed off the rock walls. He'd pinched her nipples before she'd come all the way back down sending her over a second time. *Oh sweet darlin' there is so much more I can show you. I'll make you crave my touch so much you'll never want to leave.* By the time her second orgasm wound down, her muscles were shaking from the isometric pressure of being held tight for so long. Sage helped her sit on the heated section of the bench while he finished his own shower. *Damn, that heated section of seating has to be one of Phoenix's best ideas—ever.*

Sage grabbed one of the bath sheets from the warming cabinet, and gently patted the water from her glowing skin. As he rubbed the soft towel over her hair, she stilled his hands and looked up into his eyes. "Thank you. I don't know any words to describe how amazing that felt." He smiled, and waited because he could see what was coming a mile away. "But…what about you? I mean…" Damn, if the woman blushed any brighter the whole room was going to glow like a courtesan's front porch.

"Sweetness, I'm not finished with you. Not by a long shot." He picked her up and carried her to large bed. He'd already turned down the comforter and sheet before joining her in the shower, so he settled her in the center of his large bed and followed her down. Holding himself above her, he stroked his fingers down the side of her face. "You take my breath away. You are everything I've looked for in a woman. But you need to know right now, the minute I slide my cock into your sweet heat you're going to belong to me. And I'll want it all, pet. Your pleasure will belong to me. Are you ready for that?"

According to Brandt, Coral's e-reader had provided a treasure trove of insight into the little sub lying beneath him. His brother had recited a few of the titles he'd found on the older electronic device, and Sage had been thrilled to learn about her interest in dominance and submission. Knowing he didn't have to fully explain the implications of being with a Dominant meant he was going to be able to fuck her sooner rather than later.

He'd recognized several of the authors and titles she'd chosen, he'd noted there were certain similar elements—dominance in the bedroom, spanking, flogging, exhibitionism. Yes, indeed, her tastes appeared to parallel his for the most part, but she needed to understand he would test all of her limits—regularly. He'd push her to try things she'd never imagined could bring her pleasure. Damn, he'd been relieved to find out she wasn't into hard-core pain. Sage wasn't a sadist and didn't particularly care for punishments that weren't erotic in nature. There were usually far better ways to gain compliance in his opinion. And finding out the woman he'd been giving the slow sell for months was interested in bondage was the icing on a sweet little treat laying naked under him.

Brandt had shaken his head at Sage, muttering, "I've fucking told you to check a sub's reading material. E-readers are windows into a woman's desire. You'll learn more in fifteen minutes browsing their contents list than you'll learn in months of conversation." It had been Brandt's parting shot before he'd turned and stalked back down the hall to his own suite of rooms. Each of the brothers had plans to move in to their own place on the ranch when they found a woman of their own, but for now they'd all chosen to stay close.

Refocusing his attention on the soft woman beneath him, Sage whispered against her ear, "Surrender everything to me in the bedroom and I'll show you pleasures you don't even know exist, pet. I'm going to treat you so good you'll never want to leave this house, let alone the state." He saw the tears form, but knew they weren't from sadness because her heart was right there in her eyes. He kissed the tears away, and then slowly pushed her thighs apart with his knees.

Pressing the tip of his cock against her opening, he swiveled his hips coating his tip with her juices as he let himself enjoy the wonder of the woman opening herself to him. "This is our first time together, baby, so I'm going to make love you. Then I'm going to fuck you hard and fast. I'm going to make you mine."

"Please." Her softly spoken plea was like a balm soothing his soul. It kindled a flame deep inside his chest. He closed his eyes as he fell headlong into pure bliss. Fucking hell, had anything ever felt as perfect as his bare cock sliding into her silky, wet heat? He couldn't wait to take her from behind so his hands could have free rein over her breasts. Their weight would make them bounce perfectly with each pounding thrust. He'd roll her nipples into tight peaks before giving them a firm pinch sending her deeper into the pleasure. But this time—their first together—was all about giving her a memory she'd be able to hold on to for the rest of her life. He wanted Coral to remember this moment fondly in the years to come. He wanted to be able to look into her eyes for the next fifty years and know this shared moment had brought her joy rather than pain. And more than anything else, he wanted to memorize the look on her face as she came around his cock.

I swear to you, I'm clean. And the way your heat is enveloping me, I'm never going to want anything between us, baby. Fuck, you're burning me up, pet. Your pussy is so damned hot and dripping wet. Jesus, Joseph, and sweet mother Mary, you're wrapping my cock in blazing heat and a sheath of wet silk that pulses with each beat of your heart." He was barely leashing his raging desire, every cell in his body was screaming at him to shove his cock so deep his balls slapped against her pretty pink rear hole. Christ in heaven, she was so tight he worried he'd hurt her and that was the very last thing he wanted. *Fuck, she's perfect.*

Feeling her arch instinctively beneath him, he stilled her. "No. Hold still, pet. You are so tight. We need to stretch those delicate tissues with care, sweetness." The pace was excruciatingly slow, but he was determined to ensure her safety. When he finally felt the weeping tip of his cock press against her cervix, he continued holding himself in check, letting her body take all the time it needed to adjust to his girth as he settled deep inside her. He could feel every beat of her heart and marveled at how quickly their bodies seemed to have recognized one another.

"You are so...ummm...well, you feel so huge inside of me." Sage smiled to himself and tilted his hips up slightly pulling back just a few inches before pushing deep again. Coral's eyes widened and her gasp was music to his ears. *Liked that didn't you, little subbie?* "Oh my God in heaven, it feels so amazing. But, please, please, please. I need for you to move faster...harder." An invitation straight from heaven and definitely words every Dom loves to hear. Sage was more than happy to accommodate her.

"Oh, such sweet words. I'm happy to give you what you've asked for, pet. He easily found a rhythm they both enjoyed, withdrawing slowly and then shoving deep with a hard thrust—over and over again—the movements a dance of seduction as old as time itself. With each plunge the tip of his cock pressed against her cervix, and he felt the telltale tremors of her release building. The tide of her coming orgasm shined bright in her deep blue eyes, and her heart beat wildly against his chest. Coral's dark hair was fanned around her head in a glorious tumble of damp waves, and the contrast between her hair and the color of her eyes stole his breath.

When the fluttering of her vaginal walls turned into punishing contractions he knew she was teetering on the edge, and he was right there with her. Sliding his knees up so they pressed against the backs of her thighs tilting her hips into the perfect position, he slid in fast and hard knowing the rigid corona would press against her sweet spot. She screamed before going completely wild in his arms. Sage wrapped her tightly in his embrace and in a few more strokes followed her right over the edge, free falling into a canyon that held nothing but pure white-hot rapture.

Sage was mesmerized by the colors flashing behind his eyelids and it took him several seconds to realize the shout he'd heard was his own. When he finally managed to pull enough oxygen into his lungs to speak, he looked down into her glazed expression and grinned. "You destroyed me, pet." The truth was more profound, he felt as if Coral had ripped his soul from his chest before being returning it to him—minus the small sliver she'd kept for herself. His muscles took another minute to come back to life and a couple more before he trusted his legs to hold him up. "Stay here, baby. I'll be right back."

By the time he returned with a warm washcloth and soft dry towel she was sleeping soundly. He made quick work of cleaning the evidence of their lovemaking from between her toned thighs. He gently patted her swollen tissues dry before crawling in beside her. Throwing the bed covers over them, Sage smiled at how perfectly she fit against him. The warm cocoon of blankets made him feel like they were the only two people in the world. Snuggling against his side, Coral threw her slender arm over his chest and used his shoulder as a pillow. The last thought he had before drifting off to sleep was an overpowering sense of gratitude. He'd finally found her...the woman he'd been looking for his entire life had finally found her way to him. Coral Williams fit him perfectly in every way. Her soft, warm, deliciously naked body pressed against his, settling something deep inside him. The fact she slept so contentedly told him how utterly exhausted she'd been. Knowing she trusted him enough to relax in his embrace, letting go of all the horrors she'd been dealing, with touched him clear to his soul.

# Chapter Six

CORAL WAS FLOATING somewhere between sleep and wakefulness, simply drifting on a soft cloud of expensive cotton sheets that felt more like polished silk. The pillow she was hugging smelled like Sage Morgan...*holy hell this has to be the best dream ever*. Without even moving she felt the tenderness in the tissues between her thighs as memories of the night before started to come into focus.

Letting the evening play back in her mind, she remembered when they'd been in the shower Sage told her he wanted to make their first time a memory she would cherish—and he'd done exactly that. Stretching out her tired muscles before moving from the bed, Coral was about halfway to the bathroom when the door opened and Sage stepped in to the room. She squeaked in surprise, but before she could scramble back to grab something to cover herself with, Sage pulled her into his arms. "Don't even think about hiding yourself from me, baby. There are two places in this house where you will never be allowed to cover what belongs to me—and this suite is one of those."

"One?" Coral heard the thread of doubt in her voice, and the small wrinkle between Sage's brows let her know he'd heard it as well.

"Pet, humiliation has never been my kink and I don't think it's yours either. But I do think there is a bit of exhibitionist in you, but it's something we'll need to explore." His grin was something between amused and heated desire making her want to push him...just to find out which one would win. Sage leaned down, and whispered against her ear, "Don't try to deny it, sweetness because it won't work. The great thing about this lifestyle is that you don't have to deny yourself anything. The freedom you'll find in exploring your sexuality will quickly become one of your favorite aspects of being a submissive—that is, *if* you are brave enough to take the chance."

Coral wasn't a fool—she knew a challenge when she heard one. The problem was...she didn't have any argument against what he'd said. And even if she'd had one, Coral wasn't sure she'd have voiced it. *Why would you want to limit your options, Coral Anne? This is your chance to live out a fantasy pretending you are a character in one of the books on your e-reader, even if it's only for a few days. Oh my God, I'm talking to myself again.*

CORAL TOOK TIME to explore her surroundings after lunch, and was quickly overwhelmed by the sheer size of the Morgan's home. There were literally *suites* of rooms in three different wings of the main house. She'd asked if it had once been a lodge of some kind, and Sage had laughed out loud. "No sweetness. Mama just needed a lot of space to raise five sons. I think it was how dad kept her from strangling the lot of us. To say we were a handful would be an understatement."

She'd fallen instantly in love with the sheltered area at the back of the mansion. The outdoor space was decorated for the holidays, and looked like a winter wonderland. The fading afternoon light cast the entire area in the shadows giving her a glimpse of the thousands of white lights decorating the trees and lining seating areas warmed by beautiful rock fire pits.

*Fuckalicious, I can't wait to see this at night.* There were two separate heated swimming pools connected by an arched log bridge. Coral hadn't been able to stop herself from imagining what the area must look like during the summer when the mountain meadow behind the house was painted with the bright wildflowers she'd fallen in love with last year.

"I'm pretty sure Montana is one of the places God loved most, because he sure seems to have given it all his best. The only thing missing is the ocean." Coral hadn't really intended to say the words out loud as she stared out the French doors into the frigid afternoon air. She'd enjoyed her stroll through the courtyard as Sage had called it, but the frigid temperatures had finally taken their toll. The extreme temperatures had blindsided her last winter. She'd been raised in the south, so she hadn't been prepared for the icy wind cutting through her lightweight coat. Her wardrobe was still woefully inadequate for the bitter cold she'd experienced.

Sage stepped up behind her wrapping his arm around her torso beneath her breasts. "Is that homesickness I hear in your voice, sweetness?"

"Not really. I love it here, but there is something about the ocean that resets a person's soul. The beauty of nature is displayed so abundantly. I didn't get to visit it often, but there is something about the endless rhythm of the waves making their way onto the beach that mesmerizes me."

SAGE WATCHED CORAL closely as they'd ambled through the only place he'd ever called home. He'd shown people around what had quickly become known as the Morgan Mansion more times than he could count, but Coral's reaction had been unlike most. Thinking back on Mackenzie's reaction to his home, Sage couldn't help but smile at how different the two women had reacted. Mackenzie had seen nothing but dollar signs as they'd followed much the same path he'd been taking with Coral. The woman he'd thought he was going to spend the rest of his life with had pointed out all the changes she'd be making to the house and asked more than once about the authenticity of various works of art his parents had purchased over the years— he'd known she was keeping a running tally in her head.

Jack Sorenson was one of his dad's favorite artists and there were several of his original works in what was now Sage's office. Mackenzie had wrinkled her nose in disgust. "Those are valuable? Really? Why?" When he'd tried to explain, she cut him off. "We'll sell them and find something that will work with the more modern theme we're going to incorporate throughout the house. Why anyone would want to look at pictures of sweaty cowboys is a mystery to me." Oddly enough, of all the things Mackenzie had done that should have tipped him off to their lack of compatibility—it had been that moment when Sage had finally recognized how different they really were.

Coral on the other hand hadn't once mentioned the monetary value of anything he'd shown her. But she hadn't missed the fact there were several paintings by the same artist either. The large painting over the fireplace downstairs caught her eye. "This looks like it was done by the same artist as the pictures in your office." He hadn't answered her, but simply waited while she studied the large landscape. "I didn't look at the signature...I don't really know much about art. But the feeling is the same and the use of color. It's perfect for this house. I'm not surprised you like this you know." He didn't miss the fact her words had been a statement rather than a question. *Good to know she can hold her own.*

"Explain." He hadn't meant for his response to sound gruff, but she'd surprised him and that didn't happen often.

If she'd noticed his less than polite response, she didn't comment. "It's about strength of character. All three of the pictures I think were done by the same artist have that recurring theme." Sage had been leaning against the mantle studying Coral while she'd studied the painting. When she'd looked over, meeting his gaze, he watched her eyes dilate when she realized he'd been watching her. He was convinced she hadn't intended the remarks as an attempt to gain his favor—she'd simply made an honest observation. The significance of the moment wasn't lost on him. Coral had seen right to the heart of why his dad loved Sorenson's art—something that had been completely lost on Mackenzie.

The pink tinging her cheeks made him realize he hadn't responded, and she was misinterpreting his silence. "You're exactly right, pet. And I can't tell you how thrilled Pop is going to be with your observation. You've seen right to the heart of what he loves about Sorenson's work. Not everyone sees the underlying message—they see the landscape and admire it or not. Most people don't understand the strength of character it takes to survive in such a rugged environment."

"The pictures are lovely and they fit the décor perfectly. Did your mom decorate it herself or was it done professionally?" Coral let her gaze roam around the room and Sage wanted to rejoice as he saw nothing but admiration in her expression. There was no hint of the monetary calculation he often saw when showing people around what was simply *home* to their family.

"Mom will be the first to tell you she had help redecorating a couple of years ago. But I assure you, everything you see was personally overseen by Mama Morgan. My lovely mother works like a well-oiled machine. I swear she could run the ranch with one hand tied behind her back if she put her mind to it. Take my advice—don't ever stand between Patsy Morgan and her goal, she'll steamroll you." He was pleased to see her smile at his words because her entire face lit up from the inside each time it happened. In Sage's opinion, Coral didn't smile nearly enough. But, considering everything he'd learned about her over the past twenty-four hours, he wasn't surprised. He fully intended to make it a personal mission to make her smile as often as possible—but first he needed to convince her to *stay*.

"Your home is amazing. Thank you for the tour. I should probably get my phone back from the sheriff…you know, so I can call for help if I get lost." Sage got the impression there was a bit of truth in her teasing statement. The damned place might appear vast, but with the number of people continually traipsing through, he was sure she wouldn't have trouble finding help when she needed it.

"Pet, I don't think you'll be seeing that phone again anytime soon. We'll get you a new phone soon enough. Until then, I'll keep you close enough to ensure you don't go missing." Sage closed the distance between them without hesitation, and slanted his lips over hers, sealing the gap when she gasped in surprise. The tantalizing taste of her burst through his entire system stealing his control. The kiss he'd intended as a promise of things to come rocketed straight to molten in the time it took his mind to recognize the hint of mint mixed with hefty dose of desire he identified as uniquely Coral. Each time he touched her, she stole another piece of his soul, and Sage was happy to give it up to her. He felt a growl of frustration deep in his chest when her clothing kept his hands from touching bare skin when he cupped the rounded globes of her ass and pulled her closer.

His phone vibrated in his chest pocket and Coral stepped back so quickly she stumbled. He caught her easily but quirked a brow at her in question. "Sorry, I lose my head when you kiss me. Mercy, I was ready to…ummm, well… Anyway, I forgot weren't in your suite. Holy crap on a cactus, what if someone had walked in?" *Oh my darling sub, you are going to learn there won't be a room in this house where I won't fuck you. And you can count on being seen by the other four Doms who live here—I'm going to push you to face the little inner exhibitionist I suspect lurks inside you.*

SAGE HAD SHOWN her most of the house, but had left her to explore the rest on her own while he returned to his office to take a call. She enjoyed the time alone and spent most of her time studying the family pictures lining a wide hallway on the lower level of the house. The pictures told the story of their family and it was fascinating to see how each of the brothers had changed over the years.

Coral loved the large room Sage had referred to as

their bonus room—bonus indeed, she'd seen smaller theatres. He'd told her it was their favorite place to watch movies, but hadn't been able to figure out where the heck they'd hidden the television. One entire wall of the room was made up of several sets of French doors that opened up to a sheltered patio. Whoever designed the mansion had utilized the area's uneven terrain beautifully—each of the structure's three levels had ground level access at some point. Sage had laughed when she'd mentioned it. "That's a very astute observation, sweetness. My dad insisted on that particular feature—he did raise five boys after all."

She must have looked puzzled because he snorted a laugh. "There were plenty of broken bones over the years and he didn't much like watching us going up and down the open staircase on crutches. Now that I look back on it, I think our emergency room visits were harder on him than they were on mom. Pop is a softie at heart." Sage's comments about his dad didn't surprise her at all.

Coral had waited on Sage's father, Dean Morgan, on several occasions in the hardware store. It was easy to see he held his family close to his heart. She'd been able to hear a special tenderness in his voice whenever he spoke of his sons, even if he'd been trying to act stern over something he'd been forced to replace. One day he was picking up a new winch and grinching about how his *boys* had burned out the old one pulling themselves out of a rain-swollen creek. "Damned cowboys oughta stay on their horses. Hell, a good rope is all you need then. And ropes are a damn sight cheaper than winches." She evidently hadn't looked convinced his attitude was sincere, because he'd looked down at her and grinned. "I'm bettin' you find out all about this one day soon enough. And I'm going to remind you of this conversation, darlin'—don't think I won't."

She'd almost burst into tears as the older man turned and walked out the door. It was one of those increasingly familiar moments when running again seemed like a huge mistake.

Coral felt as though her entire life had spiraled down quickly after her parents died. Losing the house had broken her heart, but witnessing a murder had shaken her to the core. The long hours driving across the country allowed her plenty of time to think about what she'd seen, and it left her little doubt she'd never really feel safe again. Coral envied the people who lived in the small Montana mountain town she'd settled into—most of them had known one another their entire lives.

It wasn't uncommon for citizens of Pine Creek to mention family associations spanning several generations. Coral wondered what it would be like to grow up with that sort of stability. Her parents hadn't been stellar citizens, but they'd been all she had. Watching "Pop" as his son's referred to him, walk out of the store that day had only underscored Coral's feelings of loneliness. A sense of sadness settled over her at the realization there was little chance she'd be able to stay in Montana long enough for Dean Morgan's prediction to come true. She must have had a wistful look on her face as Dean walked away, because when she'd looked up, Phoenix Morgan was studying her closely, his deep green eyes filled with compassion.

"He's right, you know. Hell, he's always right, but don't you dare tell him I said that." He grinned, and she knew he was trying to lighten her mood. Although she hadn't learned as much about Phoenix as she had the others, Charlotte had referred to him as "contemplative" and it was easy to see why. While he certainly *looked* every inch the hard-bodied cowboy rancher, there was a depth in his eyes that spoke of an aura of an old soul.

"I'm sure he's a very smart man, but..."

"You best keep the rest of that to yourself, sweetie. It'll save you being embarrassed about being wrong someday—of course, I'm cheating myself out of something to tease you about, but this can be your one free pass."

"Free pass?"

"Sure, every family has them. You get one mistake no one gets to hound you about." She'd laughed at him, and they'd quickly pushed it all aside as he handed over the list of office supplies he'd brought in. Because Pine Creek didn't have an office supply store, Charlotte kept a small selection of supplies in the far corner of what should probably be called a General Store rather than O'Donnell Hardware. "I know I could order these on-line, but then I wouldn't ever leave the ranch and my family already accuses me of being a recluse." She'd been grateful the subject had changed—learning all the small nuances of *normal* families always seemed to knock the wind out of her for some reason.

## Chapter Seven

THE MEMORY FROM a few months ago brought Coral's attention back to the pictures in front of her. Running her fingers along the bottom edge of the wooden frames as she worked her way through the stages of their lives. Coral admired all the different experiences the Morgan's had provided their brood over the years. It was obvious Dean and Patsy Morgan traveled the world with their five sons as they'd been growing up. There were pictures of the group visiting historically significant locations as well as more typical tourist traps. But what impressed her most were the pictures of them taken in areas of great economic need as well. *Wow. It must be wonderful to have parents willing to teach you about social responsibility rather than ways to steal from others.*

She'd been impressed with the easy smiles on the Morgan's' faces as they stood together, whether in posed vacation pictures or candid shots taken of them around the ranch. The pictures captured their lives in poignant detail. Some of the snapshots were funny while others were inspiring, but in her view the best prints were of loving parents looking on as their sons absorbed a new experience. Having been little more than a prop for her mom and dad during their frequent scams, Coral found herself longing for a connection like the one the Morgan family shared.

Glancing to the side, Coral was startled to see Colt leaning casually against the wall a few feet from her. Stifling her gasp, she'd slapped her hand against her chest, "Holy crap on a cracker. You scared the canaries right out of me."

His quick bark of laughter surprised her. "Canaries, huh? Because they sing so easily? Meaning I scared the words from you?" She felt her eyes go wide...people so rarely understood that expression, and she couldn't help being impressed. "Aha, I see I've surprised you. Didn't think the rodeo boy had any smarts?"

"What? Why on earth would you think such a thing? I just happen to know it's an odd expression and really I've found people rarely understand it. I'm actually quite impressed." And she was. Her mother had often used the expression, and though Coral tried very hard to break habits she felt linked her to her parents, sometimes things slipped right past all those lovely filters she'd set in place. *Damn.*

"No worries, darlin', but it actually happens a lot—the underestimation of my intelligence, I mean—so I'm probably paranoid. Seems the general public doesn't hold professional bull riders in much intellectual esteem."

Coral had purposely let herself study Colt Morgan for several seconds, she wanted him to know she was considering her words carefully. "I'd guess that's a mistake on their part. Seems to me you'd have to be pretty smart to survive intact long enough to even make it to the professional level of such a demanding sport. I've watched it on television a few times. I've always been amazed at the balance and reflexes involved—nothing is ever the same twice and it happens so very quickly. That sort of skill set is only developed after a lot of well-thought out training." She saw his cheeks flush ever so slightly at the compliment, before she continued, "And I'd be willing to wager painful experience is a good teacher as well."

Colt leaned his head back and laughed. "Damn, beautiful and smart. Sage hit the jack pot." Then it had been her turn to blush. "Don't be embarrassed and don't you dare argue with me. I'll rat you out and get that pretty little behind of yours a swat or two." His words brought back a flood of deliciously heated memories. Coral's mind slid right back to the moment Sage's rock hard body had pressed her much smaller frame to the wall of the master suite's shower a few hours earlier. Sage hadn't hurt her, but he'd used enough pressure to ensure she wasn't going to move without a struggle. Knowing he'd essentially bound her with nothing but his chest pressing against her back and one hand wrapped around her crossed wrists sent a wash of her creamy arousal racing to coat her softening sex. *Just like it is now remembering it.*

Coral's attraction to Sage Morgan had been growing steadily over the past year to the point she'd been worried she wouldn't be able to contain it much longer. Holy hell, she'd had daydreams about launching herself into his arms as he walked down the hardware store's back aisles. *You'd have looked like a spider monkey trying to get King Kong's attention. So not cool, Coral Ann.*

Sage's whispered words floated through her mind as she'd stood in the hall staring blankly at Colt. As he'd pressed against her, Sage's warm breath had caressed the shell of her ear as the water cascaded down around them. "I'm a Dom, pet." His pause had been long enough for her to absorb the information, but not long enough for her to respond before he pushed his erection between the apex of her thighs making her gasp in need. She already been slick and ready, and all she wanted was to feel him pushing deep into her sex. But he'd seemed content to continue the conversation—*blasted man.*

When Sage had finally continued, it had taken her several seconds to mentally tune back in to what he was saying, because her mind was focused on how delicious it felt to have his hot flesh pressing against the swollen folds of her pussy. "But you already knew that didn't you?" *Huh? Knew that?* "There is always a part of one's soul that knows…a part that recognizes the kindred spirit of another who is like-minded. We're going to have a long conversation about your interests and experience, but not right now. Right now I'm going to claim what belongs to me. I'm going to fuck you so deep you'll know I've planted a piece of my soul deep inside you." *Now we're talking.*

When she blinked back to the moment, Coral saw a smile tugging at the corners of Colt's lips. "Damn, but I'd love to know what just went through your mind, sweetness." Before she could blunder through a lie, Colt had shaken his head. "Don't even try to come up with a cover story—it won't work. But know this, *that* is a look *every* Dom recognizes, sweet girl. I was sure my brother had laid his cards on the table pretty quickly. This is something you can count on in this family and in the lifestyle, Coral—we'll always level with you. *Always.* You can trust Sage…you can trust all of us. We'll keep you safe, even if it means keeping you safe from yourself." *Uh oh…that sounds a bit ominous.*

As Colt stepped in the back door he'd seen Sage heading into his office, a frown creasing his brow. His older brother look annoyed, something Colt hadn't expected. As the eldest of the Morgan brothers, Sage had always taken the responsibility of that position far too seriously even as a child. But now? Hell, it wasn't as if the rest of them hadn't grown into competent adults fully capable of taking some of the enormous burden from his shoulders. Okay, maybe Kip hadn't fully morphed into the man they all knew he would be, but Sage wasn't doing a thing to help the kid along either. Treating him like a college frat-rat instead of a partner in the business wasn't going to help Kim mature—and the kid had enormous potential as a ranch manager.

Colt knew Sage had been pussy footing around Coral Williams for months. Why he'd been so reluctant to make a direct move mystified everyone, because it was totally out of character for the man who'd grabbed the reins of a fifty thousand acre ranch without blinking. The same man who oversaw several small mines, as well as their family's varied other business interests without breaking a sweat, wasn't hesitant. So his stand-down approach had baffled those who knew him best. Hell, the eldest among them had reached Master status as a trained sexual Dominant before he'd been old enough to drink legally at the fucking clubs the two of them had frequented. But a tiny newcomer working at the local hardware store had launched the *confident, professional* Sage they'd all come to know right out the window. In his place? A growling bear emerged. Hell, even their mama had been threatening mutiny.

The first week after their parents returned before Thanksgiving to spend the holiday season in Montana, Colt had seen his mother stomping down the sidewalk downtown. Patsy Morgan stomping mad was never a good sign, so Colt had quickly pulled over to find out who he was going to need to forewarn.

"What's up, mama? You don't look any too happy.

Who do I need to bust-up so I get to see your sweet smile again?" Colt asked when he finally caught up with her. He'd fallen into step beside her and grinned at her slower-than-normal pace. He'd fought to hold back his grin because no doubt it had been her fashionable spike-heeled boots that had slowed her pace.

"Colt Morgan don't you patronize me. If I tell you who put this frown on my face you'll warn them I'm coming—I know about *the network*, don't you think I don't." *Holy shit! Who the hell told her about that?* Their dad had implemented "the mama network" years ago—most likely it had been a way to keep his wife from dwindling down the number of their offspring. If one of the brothers knew their dad or a sibling was facing a tongue lashing or worse from "the force" as their dad often referred to his wife—then that "man" was obligated to warn the target. "Your daddy isn't as sneaky as he thinks he is. How you all thought you were keeping it under your hats was almost comical, but it didn't serve my purpose to bust you out on it. But that brother of yours—his hide is mine, and I'm not gonna do a thing to help you warn him."

"Well, mama that would be tough since I don't know which one of them has offended you."

Colt had been sure his words were well chosen, but she turned on him anyway. "Boy, oh boy, you really do think I'm a dim-wit don't you, Colt Morgan?"

"Um…no ma'am." *Fuck, this is going downhill fast. Wonder which one of those damned brothers of mine has jumped into it feet first this time?*

"Impossible. The whole lot of you are purely impossible. I swear I'm getting a plane ticket and flying back south. You all can eat bologna sandwiches on Thanksgiving for all I care."

"Damn, mama. That's just plain old mean-spirited. You know you're the best cook this side of the Rockies, we're all looking forward to Thanksgiving." Okay, that was really pushing it. Patsy was a decent enough cook, but she'd also incinerated her share of beef over the years too. His dad had always laughed, and said there were plenty more steaks in the freezer. They'd sure eaten dinner late on many occasions because their mother had gotten distracted while grilling.

But today there didn't seem to be any way to distract her and she hadn't taken the bait. "Lame, Colt. Very, very lame." He'd followed her into the diner, and then watched as she'd zeroed in on Sage. Colt hadn't seen that one coming and had almost turned around to leave his grumpy brother to his fate—as it turned out, Colt had been happy he'd decided to stick around. It was fun seeing his brother sweat bullets after dealing with his cranky-ass nonsense for months.

Their mom had proceeded to rip Sage into little pieces about his recent "bout of idiocy," and the way he'd been treating everyone within a hundred miles according to their mom's morning coffee posse. Evidently Patsy's friends had been more than happy to regale her with tale after tale of Sage's recent outbursts, and Mama Morgan was none too pleased with her oldest child. She'd finally wound down enough to actually fall into a chair and lean close. "You listen to me, Sage Morgan. This all about that sweet girl down at the hardware store—I know full well it is, so don't you be trying any of your smoke and mirrors tricks with me. You either ask that sweet girl out or walk away because you are making everybody miserable and none of us need it, least of all Coral." With that she'd stood up and marched right back out the door to the claps and whistles of everyone within hearing range. Hell, Colt had cheered as loud as anyone else in the room.

And now, it looked like the grumpy bear was back in residence. *Yippee fucking skippy.* Sage waved him over, excusing himself from whoever he'd been speaking with on the phone long enough to direct Colt to the lower level. "Coral is downstairs looking around. Make sure she doesn't get into trouble." His brother's raised brow wasn't needed, Colt knew exactly what *trouble* his brother was trying to avoid. Their playroom was downstairs. It wasn't that any of them were ashamed of the lifestyle they'd chosen, but today wasn't the day to introduce her to their dungeon.

When he'd first found her downstairs, Colt leaned against a doorframe watching Coral study each picture with admiration, and something very close to longing in her pretty eyes. He'd read the report Brandt put together on the brunette beauty, and knew nothing in her life had been easy. Colt felt a twinge of guilt when he considered how idyllic his and his brothers' lives had been while Coral had encountered nothing but rocks, boulders, and detours along life's path. And just now, when he'd mentioned tattling on her to get her a swat or two he'd been shocked by her reaction. She'd immediately flushed and then zoned out—he didn't know exactly where she'd gone, but he had a pretty good idea what—*or at least who*, was playing through her mind. The entire scene had been fascinating to watch, and Colt couldn't remember a time when he'd wished more for the ability to read someone's mind. Damn, he'd have loved to able to see whatever Coral had been seeing in her mind's eye.

"Tell me, sweetness, until last night—how long had it been since you'd slept a whole night through?" Colt saw her eyes widen before pink painted her cheeks, and he couldn't hold back his grin. "Don't be embarrassed, it was a safe bet my brother would make sure you were exhausted enough to sleep, sweetheart. He's wanted you in his bed for a long time." She was going to have to get used to the fact none of the Morgan brothers would pull any punches with her—it simply wasn't the way they were wired. They were all members of at least one kink club, though some of them were definitely more dedicated to their roles as Doms than others.

Colt watched her take a mental step back—it was written clearly in her body language. Under ordinary circumstances, he would have been forced to allow her attempt to hide because she didn't belong to him. But, Sage had silently slipped back into the room, standing behind her, he'd nodded his head for Colt to continue. "Again I'll remind you of the importance of honesty, sweetness. I believe you will find Doms are fairly rigid about that particular rule—and remember, honesty applies to *all things* for some very good reasons. You'll learn all the reasons as you learn more about the lifestyle." He gave her a few seconds to process what he'd said before continuing, "Now, answer my question. How long?"

She'd met his gaze, but only long enough to convince him she wasn't planning to lie—she was simply embarrassed to be put on the spot. Likely she wasn't accustomed to other people looking out for her, even though he knew Charlotte had been mothering her as much as the independent young woman would allow. *May as well get it over with, baby. I'm not going anywhere and your Master is losing patience with every breath.*

Taking a deep breath as if stealing herself for his anger, Coral finally sighed, "Several weeks. The thing is, I really like it here, but I haven't managed to save much money after spending so much to fix my car." Colt didn't even want to think about what it had cost her to get the death trap she'd been driving back into working order—probably far more than it had been worth.

"Is there a reason you hadn't spoken to Brandt about the problems you were having?"

This time she took an actual step back, her eyes going wide. "Well, yes, actually there is. If you think about it, I'm a material witness to a murder. Not something most law enforcement personnel feel you should run from." Colt wanted to laugh out loud because she'd absolutely nailed it. "And your brother doesn't really appear to be the understanding type, if you know what I mean." Oh yeah, he certainly understood what she meant.

"Why not speak to Sage? You had to know he was interested in you."

She didn't answer for so long he wondered if she planned to simply ignore the inquiry. When she finally returned her gaze to his, Colt felt a jolt of electricity pierce his heart at the stark look of longing in her eyes. God in heaven, he hoped someday he'd find a treasure of his own like the one standing in front of him. His brother better pull this off because Coral Williams wore her heart on her sleeve and she was obviously genuine all the way to her soul. "That's exactly why I *didn't tell him*."

In many ways, Colt understood Coral's line of thinking—but it didn't mean he agreed with her. But just to be sure *his brother* understood, Colt pushed on. "I'm not sure I understand exactly what that means. So—as Sage would say…*clarify*." Colt had the advantage of standing face to face with her. He could see her expressions up close, but Sage was looking over his shoulder. Colt knew Sage was trying to see as much as possible in the mirror on the opposite wall without drawing Coral's notice.

Coral took what Colt recognized as a fortifying breath before looking up from where her eyes had dropped. "Sage is a well-respected businessman, Colt. He doesn't need to be caught up in this mess." *Oh sweetheart you just bought yourself a whole lot of trouble.* Colt was barely able to bite back his smile. Holy shit, his brother was about to blow a fuse. Colt hoped Sage didn't have a stroke before this conversation was over.

He didn't respond, Colt simply waited for her to continue. "Geez Louise, you're gonna play dense, huh?"

The Dom in Colt surged to the surface. "Careful, sweetness. You'd be well advised to remember Sage isn't the only Dom in the family." Her soft gasp assured him she understood exactly what he'd meant.

"I'm not trying to be disrespectful, but you and I both know exactly what I meant. I don't know why I have to say it out loud. The reputation of your entire family could be tarnished by this, and I don't want to be responsible for it. And God forbid something happened to one of you. Your entire family would end up resenting me, and it would break my heart to know I could have kept you safe if I'd just walked away." She'd spoken the last part so softly Colt wondered if Sage had been able to hear her. Sage's expression softened, and Colt knew he'd caught every word.

"Before I turn you over to Sage, I want to make something clear, sweetness. Families don't back you when everything is easy. Hell, you don't *need* a family when the sea ahead of you is smooth sailing. The real strength of *this family* is in our commitment to each other when things go to hell."

Coral's pretty blue eyes filled with tears as Sage's arms wrapped around her from behind. Colt watched his brother lean down, his lips so close to Coral's ear she would feel the words as well as hear them. "Listen to what Colt is telling you, love. My brothers and I will always tell you the truth. Do you really think our family would have the reputation for doing the *right thing* if we walked away from people who are important to us just because it might get messy?"

The first tear trailed down her cheek, and Colt felt his heart clinch. "I don't really know much about how *normal families* work. When I was growing up a teacher at school knew my parents. She also knew how embarrassed I was by everything my mom and dad had done to people in our community." Colt stood perfectly still watching as his brother turned Coral so she faced him. Sage's expression was one of compassion and interest without an ounce of judgment, and Colt couldn't remember a time when he'd been more proud of his older brother.

"Mrs. Fischer told me I didn't have to follow my parents' example…that I could build my own reputation. She taught me how a good reputation could be my most valuable possession and it wouldn't cost me anything. When I found out I could have something of value without being forced to steal money to get it…well, that made a very big impression, you know?"

"How old were you, baby?" Sage's voice had an underlying edge Colt hoped Coral hadn't noticed. Colt knew his brother was skating along the edge of blind rage. Every protective instinct Sage had spent years honing as he dealt with four younger brothers would pale in comparison to what Colt knew Sage would feel for Coral.

Sage was fighting an internal battle unlike any he'd ever known. A part of him wanted to rage at the injustice of Coral's childhood. But another part of him wanted to rejoice at the woman she'd become. Her inner strength humbled him, and he found himself admiring her more with each passing minute. Her quiet response shocked him. "Seven. But I'd been forced to grow up pretty quickly. I wasn't like most kids my age in a lot of ways." *No fucking doubt, sweetheart.*

Colt shook his head in disbelief as he quietly slipped away, leaving Sage alone with the woman he hoped would stay after the danger to her passed. He could only hope after tomorrow night's party she understood how much he cared for her. He'd assigned each of his family members tasks related to the surprises he had in store for her. Sage had planned to take Coral on a tour of the ranch after lunch, but maybe it was time for a bit of distraction. Switching gears, giving her something else to think about for a while, might be more fun for both of them.

"I want you to know how incredibly impressed I am, baby. You've overcome obstacles that would have caused most people to implode. You're so much stronger than you realize. I'm proud of you." A fresh stream of tears made their way down her soft cheeks, but Sage knew these weren't tears from pent up emotional pain. No, these were tears of emotional grounding, and he was happy to have given her a small taste of what it would be like to have an anchor in the storm. "No matter what happens between us, Coral—I'll always be in your corner. I don't want you to ever forget it. We may not always agree—hell, I can promise you we won't always agree. But I can also promise you I'll always have your best interest at heart."

Leaning down, Sage pressed a kiss to the center of her

forehead, and then wrapped his arms around her. Hugging her—just the very simple act of holding her close brought about an unexpected peace. When he felt the tension fade from her petite frame, he wanted to shout out his thanks for the opportunity to finally have her in his home. It was time to lighten the mood and Sage had an idea he hoped would also be a fun way to find out exactly how daring his little sub could be.

## Chapter Eight

Sage watched Coral's eyes widen when he stepped back and gave her a look he knew was different from the one she was accustomed to seeing. "I want to change directions, sweetness. You've been reading about dominance and submission, so the terminology is familiar to you, isn't it?" Her wide eyes were fast becoming a deeper shade of green as they dilated letting him know arousal was eclipsing the emotional turmoil she'd been reeling in a few minutes earlier.

When she finally nodded, he shook his head. "Sweetness, you need to answer with words. And we've already begun, so be sure to answer appropriately."

Damn she was going to destroy his control—she was so fucking responsive, he wanted to skip all the buildup and push her against the nearest wall and lose himself inside her. "Yes, Sir."

"Perfect. You please me more than you know, pet. Now, I'm going to escort you upstairs. I've got a small gift to give you before we have lunch. My gift is going to set the stage for what we'll be doing after we've finished eating. But before we go, remove your shoes." She looked puzzled, but quickly slipped off her shoes and handed them to him. If he had his way her worn out canvas shoes would disappear forever. How on earth she'd managed to make a single pair of cloth shoes last an entire year in Montana was un-fucking-imaginable. "Now, come along. I'm anxious to get started."

When they reached the main floor of the house, Sage could hear his brothers in the kitchen. He knew his parents hadn't made it back from Billings yet, so he stopped Coral at the bottom of the stairs. "Face me, pet." When she complied, he smiled. "Hand me your shirt and bra." She gasped, but her eyes sparkled with arousal as she tried to look around him into the kitchen. "If you stall I'll take you into the kitchen and we'll start again there." Her hands quickly found the bottom hem of her shirt pulling it quickly over her head before handing it to him. Her bra's front closure snapped open revealing taut nipples already turning a deep rose as blood rushed into the pretty peaks.

"You take my breath away." Sage trailed his fingers down the slope of first one breast and then the other before giving her nipples each a gentle pinch.

"Well, this is a lovely surprise," Phoenix's voice sounded from the wide door opening into the family room beside him. Coral yelped in surprise, her hand coming up to cover her breasts.

"No, don't hide. You are beautiful. Don't you dare hide what belongs to me." He hadn't planned to push her quite this quickly, but of all his brothers, Phoenix was the best suited to help her get through the next few minutes.

"Darlin' we're all Doms. I promise you, if your Master didn't want me to enjoy this view or he thought you wouldn't enjoy this moment—none of us would be standing here." Sage watched her eyes go from alarmed to full-on arousal in the span of a few seconds. Her breathing sped up and he could see her pulse pounding at the base of her neck as the telltale blush of arousal spread over her chest. *Fucking perfect.*

"She's beautiful isn't she? But if she doesn't move those hands back to her sides she's going to find herself over my knee right here in the front hall." There were several upholstered benches along the large room's periphery, finding a spot to follow through on the promise he'd just made would be no problem at all.

"And I'm sure the sound of the palm of Sage's hand paddling your bare ass will draw an audience pretty quickly. Baby doll, you might want to move your hands right *now*." Sage didn't even try to hold back his grin when her hands dropped before her mind could have possibly processed Phoenix's command. She'd responded to his brother's tone of voice before the order itself had registered. *Such a purely submissive response.* For the first time since Sage had noticed Phoenix standing to his side, his brother's eyes found his own, his expression easy to read. Sage agreed, she was fucking perfect.

Reaching forward, Sage brushed the tips of his fingertips over the very tips of her tightly peaked nipples, smiling when they drew up impossibly tighter. "You really are so very responsive, pet. I can hardly wait to tie you to my bed and explore every inch of you." He was anxious to introduce her to so many different aspects of the lifestyle, including the joys of having more than one pair of hands providing for her pleasure. And if her reaction to Phoenix's presence was anything to judge by, she was more than a little interested in the prospect.

"Tell me brother, what are your plans for your delectable little subbie?" Damn if he didn't want to turn and give his brother a fucking high five, the man could anticipate during a scene like no other. Phoenix had set him up perfectly.

"I'm taking her upstairs to decorate her a bit before

lunch. Then I think we might take a swim, it'll give her a chance to relax a bit before tomorrow's chaos." Once their parents returned home, Sage knew he'd have to minimize Coral's risk of exposure. His parents might practice D/s in private, but they'd always been careful to keep all traces of nudity carefully hidden from their sons. Hell, Sage had only discovered their interest in the lifestyle because he'd returned home late one afternoon and found them deeply immersed in a bondage scene downstairs.

Sage had been terrified when he'd first heard the sound of the single tail whip his father had been using. He'd quickly realized his mother wasn't screaming in pain from the lashes, the sounds she'd been making were anything but cries for help. Sage remembered being frozen in place for several seconds before having the presence of mind to back up the stairs before he'd been seen. It wasn't until months later he learned his father had known he was there. *And wasn't that an interesting conversation? Nothing awkward about having your dad chat you up about the importance of letting people know you're on your way home from college a day early. Christ!* Yeah, surprises weren't all they were cracked up to be in the Morgan household, that was for sure.

"Might want to get a move on then, lunch is almost ready," Phoenix's voice brought Sage back to the present, and he almost cringed when he realized Coral was searching his expression. No doubt she was wondering what she'd done wrong to merit his silence. Sage would thank his brother later for the *save*. Right now he needed to get her upstairs and naked so he could remind her how much he admired her bravery.

"Noted. Let's go, pet. I have plans for you before we enjoy whatever my brothers have come up with for lunch." As soon as they were at the top of the sweeping staircase,

Sage pulled her to a stop. The master suite was at the other end of the long hall, and despite Phoenix's warning Sage had no desire to rush back downstairs. "Give me the rest of your clothing, baby. I want to watch you walk down the hall naked. I'm going to enjoy the view while I decide exactly how I want to *decorate* you before lunch."

Damn he loved the way her eyes went wide with surprise before glossing over with a carnal delight even a novice Dom would recognize. He didn't take his eyes off hers, but the unmistakable sound of her zipper being lowered let him know she was already complying. Seconds later she handed him her folded jeans. He'd smiled when she tried to tuck her plain cotton panties into the pocket of her Levis without him seeing them. He'd warned her they were going to disappear—and they were, starting now. His mom would bring her plenty of lacy bits of nothing tomorrow, but until then he planned to make sure Coral's pretty pink bits were exposed and ready for his touch.

Watching her pert ass walk down the hall would go down as one of his all-time best fantasies come to life. Fucking perfect. He'd caught up with her before she reached the door. He placed his palm over the dimples just above her ass, and the jolt of electricity racing up his arm at the contact caught him off guard. "You've just fulfilled one of my favorite fantasies, pet. Now let's see about checking another off the list before we join the others for lunch."

CORAL'S ENTIRE BODY was vibrating with need, a desire so intense it was quickly overshadowing her every inhibition. She might not fully understand everything that had happened in the last few minutes, but there was no mistaking the way her body craved Sage's touch. The evidence of her arousal was so thick between the folds of her bare pussy, Coral worried he'd see rivulets running down the insides of her thighs before she'd reached the door of the master suite. Once inside, Coral found herself wondering exactly what she was supposed to do, and the look on her face must have given away her because when she looked up, Sage was watching her so closely his gaze felt like a physical caress.

"Tell me what you're thinking, pet." His voice was deeper, more commanding than she was accustomed to hearing and it left no doubt that his words weren't simply a request.

Coral didn't look into his eyes for fear she'd see the disappointment she'd seen in her parents' eyes so often as a child. "I don't know what to do. I hate not knowing what I'm supposed to do. Really, I'm usually very compliant…okay, maybe I should say often instead of usually." *Stop babbling and get on with it for craps-sake.*

"Look at me, Coral." Her eyes snapped to his immediately, and she was relieved to see nothing but compassion in his expression. "First of all, thank you for trusting me enough to tell me exactly what put the strained look on your face—because the only way for me to help you work through this is for you to be completely honest in all things. I can't solve a problem I don't know about." She felt some of the tension drain from her shoulders simply because what he'd said made perfect sense to her. "Now, I know you've read a lot of erotic titles, did you notice a recurring theme for the submissives? Something they consistently mentioned as a benefit of a D/s relationship?"

Coral knew immediately where Sage was leading her with his questions. And even though she knew he was pushing her toward the answer, Coral was grateful he was letting her sort it out in her mind. She knew her own limitations, and now it seemed Sage understood them as well. "Pet?" He didn't seem frustrated with her for not answering immediately, he was just pulling her back to the moment.

"They always mention how free they felt because they didn't need to worry about what they should do next. In most of the books I read, all they needed to do in the bedroom was follow orders." Coral knew she'd blurted out all the words so quickly it might not have even made sense, but Sage's smile told her he'd understood perfectly.

He'd wrapped his large hand around the base of her skull, tilting her face up to his. "This is on me, pet—not you. I've been negligent in setting the ground rules. Hell, we should have a long conversation about hard and soft limits before we even thought about playing. But this isn't a club hook-up. You are far more important and the truth is, I simply couldn't wait to make you mine." Coral felt her body react to the declaration, she felt like every cell was being switched on—lighting her up from the inside.

"Ummm…can I ask a question?"

"Always. There may come a time when that will change, but that is a long time coming, sweetness. For now, as long as you are respectful, I will encourage you to ask questions. We'll both benefit from clear communication."

"What's down the hall on the bottom floor no one wants me to see?"

## Chapter Nine

For a split second Sage was convinced all of the oxygen had suddenly been sucked out of the room. He'd been so blindsided by Coral's question, his mind scrambled for an answer, he came up empty making every second to feel like an eternity. His hand was still wrapped around the back of her neck, and he felt his fingers flex against her bare skin making her hair rasp over the back of his hand. The soft sensation startled him back to the moment, and he smiled down at her. *Fuck me, I should have known she'd figure it out.* "The play room is just down the hall from where I left you. It's locked, but I didn't want you to become concerned about what might be concealed behind a locked door."

"Play room? Like a dungeon? A personal version of what they have at sex clubs?" He heard a thread of fear in her voice and wanted to groan in frustration—this had been exactly what he'd tried to avoid.

"Yes. But you aren't ready for that yet. You might not ever be ready for it." When her eyes started to shine with unshed tears, he cursed his poor handling of the situation. The last thing he wanted to do was give her cause to question whether or not they were right for one another. "Don't worry about any of this, baby. We'll work it out." Using his hold on her to expose the side of her neck, Sage took advantage of the position by running his tongue over the sensitive skin behind her ear. Gooseflesh raced over her skin and he smiled to himself at the shiver he felt race through her. Coral was amazingly responsive and he could hardly wait to bind her. Hell, he'd already purchased enough rope for her to last months if not years. He'd dreamt of spending hours tying each knot as she slipped further and further into subspace.

"Now, be a good girl and lie back on the bed." He helped her sit at the edge of the bed but didn't let her scoot far from the edge. "No, keep that beautiful ass of yours right here, now raise your legs and place your heels on the edge of the mattress." Sage wanted to laugh at the horrified look on her face. She was going to become accustomed to such exposure—in a big hurry. It always amazed him when subs suddenly became shy about exposing themselves to their Doms. Hell, he'd seen women do public scenes completely open to an entire roomful of people, and then have a meltdown an hour later in a private room when asked to spread themselves for their Dom. *Baffling.*

They'd already been upstairs longer than he'd planned, and he didn't want to miss lunch with his brothers since their presence was needed for the lesson he'd planned for her. Without hesitation, Sage slipped a small clit ring into his mouth before kneeling down so his face was inches from the smooth lips of her pussy. The soft folds were swelling beautifully, turning the pink tissues a shade just this side of magenta. "I have a small gift for you. You'll wear it under the pretty blue sundress I saw hanging in the closet. But baby, this little ring and that sweet dress are the only things you'll be wearing to lunch today." He didn't give her a chance to respond before he began what could only be considered an all-out oral assault on her pink nub.

Coral arched her back pressing her slick folds against

his chin in an effort to control the stimulation. Sage spread his palm over her lower abdomen holding her in place. The span of his hand wrapped her from one side to the other emphasizing the difference in their size. *Great God, she is a tiny little thing.* As Sage's respect for Coral grew, his view was taking on larger than life proportions and he often forgot how petite she really was. Drawing out his sweet clit was easy because she was so very responsive. Before she realized what was happening, he'd slipped the small gold ring around the pink bundle of nerves. The ring was actually two gold circles nestled together, and when they were rotated the two locked together keep a sub's clit from retreating beneath its hood. The constant stimulation would keep Coral on edge through lunch and add a whole new dimension to their afternoon swim.

Pulling away from her, Sage chuckled when she shrieked in frustration. "Soon, baby. Very soon. Right now it's time for lunch." Wrapping his hand around her wrist, Sage pulled Coral to her to her feet. Leaning down to press kisses along her shoulder, he spoke against her soft skin, "And remember, you aren't allowed to come without permission."

Leading her to the closet where he'd hung her dress, Sage held it out to her, enjoying the view as she dropped the soft cotton dress over her head. It certainly wasn't a dress you'd expect to see a woman wear during a Montana winter, but he was confident she would be warm enough in the house. He'd be willing to bet his younger brother had already turned up the heat a degree or two knowing Coral was going to be dressed scantily when they returned to the kitchen.

They were halfway down the hall when Sage heard Coral groan. "What's the matter, pet?"

"Oh...ummm, nothing." *Really? Sure sounded like something to me.*

"Lying has consequences, pet." By the time they reached the top of the front staircase Coral's cheeks were flushed and her respiration had already accelerated. Sage walked down the first few steps before turning to face her. He wanted to be face to face so he could better gauge how she was tolerating the stimulation. He'd seen submissives climax after walking short distances, and he certainly didn't want her coming while walking down a long, open stairway. "I'll ask you again, is anything wrong?

This time her chin tilted up, and he was pleased to see tenacity shining in her eyes. The message was clear. *You want my submission? You'll have to earn it.* Sage felt a surge of gratitude, damn there wasn't much in the world he loved more than a challenge. *Game on, baby.*

Watching as Coral tried to bring her body back under control, Sage kept her wrist encircled in his grip, letting the tips of his fingers feather over her pounding pulse. Her heart was racing and if she didn't manage to slow it down soon he knew he'd be forced to remove the clit ring. It would take time to learn what she could tolerate. There would be a lot of trial and error since she wasn't an experienced submissive so she wasn't able to assess her limits either. It was a vicious cycle, but not insurmountable.

"Not *wrong* really, I'm just trying to figure out why my whole body feels like it's on fire. I can't think straight and my legs feel like they aren't connected to my body. Why is that? Something isn't right. I don't know if I can do what you want—what if I'm no good at this? What's wrong with me? Here I am talking like you'd even consider keeping me and that's insane."

He watched in wonder as her face flushed and a crashing wave of release blindsided her. Sage was already reaching for her when she started looking into the air around her. "Oh my fucking God." Coral's entire body tensed as shudders moved in small waves through her muscles. She'd shouted his name a split second before she began weaving back and forth. "Do you see those dots?" *No, baby—that's you hyperventilating.* He'd no sooner gotten his arms around her than she dropped like a stone.

"Bring her on down. She'll be alright, you just let her go too long. Classic new sub reaction—what did you put on her? Clamps or clit ring?" Colt's voice sounded from the bottom of the stairs, and Sage wasn't surprised one of his brothers had heard Coral's small outburst since her speech had gotten louder and faster the longer she'd talked. Oddly enough, he found his brother's presence comforting rather than intrusive. Sage knew full well there were times when another set of eyes and ears were vital to maximizing a submissive's experience—there were so many things to focus on, and one Dom could easily miss something important during a scene.

The brothers had often discussed the advantages of sharing women, but ultimately they'd all decided occasional ménage scenes were as far as they'd be willing to go. They had friends who were in polyamorous marriages, but that wasn't something Sage had felt was right for him. And now he'd finally gotten Coral into his bed, he knew he was far too possessive of her to share more than occasional scenes designed to enhance her pleasure.

"Clit ring, but she was already spun up pretty high before I got it into place. I told her she wasn't allowed to come. Damn it, I knew she wasn't experienced enough to hold off an orgasm." He hadn't given her permission to come because he'd wanted her on edge during lunch—in hindsight it had been a big mistake. She wasn't experienced enough to rein in her desire. He suspected she was like most naturally submissive women in vanilla relationships, if you got close to a *real* orgasm, you chased it for all it was worth because those relationships just didn't get you where you needed to go. He'd talked to many women who'd told him how unfilled they'd been prior to finding their way into the lifestyle.

Knowing he'd made her feel insecure made him feel like an ass—it had been the last thing he'd wanted to do. Even though he'd known her for a year, she had only been in his bed for less than twenty-four hours. *You're rushing this and you'll lose her if you aren't careful.* "Hey, big brother—don't even go there." Colt's voice jarred him out of his thoughts and into motion.

Sage carried her down the stairs, making his way into the kitchen. He settled her on his lap, and when he felt her tensing in his arms he knew she was starting to come back to herself. He also knew what his brother's warning meant. Colt had been cautioning Sage to steer clear of the guilt threating to consume him. The rational part of his mind knew it wouldn't serve any purpose, but his heart wasn't listening.

All he'd ever wanted was a love like the one he saw in his father's eyes when he looked at his mother—and he'd nearly let Mackenzie destroy that dream. Coral had rekindled his hope and knowing he'd made her doubt her ability to please him was ripping his heart in two. "I'm sorry." Her whispered words had been so quiet, Sage might have missed them if he hadn't felt the warmth of her breath move over the thin cotton shirt he wore.

Pressing a kiss to the top of her head, he took a deep

breath trying to calm himself before speaking. She needed him to be in control because it was clear she was feeling anything but. Soul crushing arousal and the feeling she'd let him down by coming without permission would have been enough to push many subs over the edge. He'd also managed to layer those over the exhaustion and fear she'd been experiencing the past few weeks—*fuck*. Sighing at his own selfish behavior, Sage wasn't surprised to see the look of reproof he was getting from Phoenix.

The next to youngest among them stood at the end of the kitchen counter, his bulging arms crossed over his broad chest. Phoenix might spend hours in front of a bank of computers but it didn't keep the man from spending an impressive number of hours in the state of the art gym they'd built on site. Sage knew Phoenix rivaled Brandt in that regard and God knew the good Sheriff was still operating in Navy SEAL mode when it came to physical training. Heaven help the women who took those two on.

"Look at me, pet." When she didn't move, Sage leaned back and tipped her face to his, and looked down into pretty green eyes swimming in tears. "What happened at the top of the stairs wasn't your fault—all the responsibility lies with me, sweetheart. I have been pushing you—I've been damned selfish and I want to apologize." When her eyes widened in surprise, Sage couldn't help but laugh. "Oh baby, just because I'm a Dom doesn't mean I won't make mistakes. And as you can see…" He used his hand to make a sweeping motion indicating her needed to look around the room. "There are several men here who are more than happy to ensure my accountability—particularly as it pertains to you."

"Damn straight," Colt's voice sounded from beside him as Phoenix and Kip expressed similar sentiments.

"Consider them your knights in shining armor. Our family is close, baby, and a big part of that bond is our willingness to tell one another the truth. When one of us is fucking up we don't hesitate to point it out. But we also back one another and offer our love and support to correct any problems we see."

"Case in point—Brandt still struggles with the effects of PTSD at times. It isn't as bad now as it was when he first left the SEALs, and frankly I'm not sure he'll ever be the same man who left home when he was nineteen," Colt's voice was steady as he skirted a subject all four of them had worried over for too long.

Phoenix nodded. "And even though we knew the experience would change him—hell, I can't imagine seeing war and not being changed by it, it doesn't mean we were willing to accept all of the challenges those changes presented. We've put his ass on the hot seat so many times for his harsh behavior it's a wonder his backside didn't burn to a crisp." Sage and his brothers all chuckled at the truth of Phoenix's remark.

Kip stepped closer and knelt in front of Coral, wrapping her slender fingers in his own. "What we're dancing around here, princess, is the fact we know Sage is moving too fast, but we also know why he's doing it. We'll kick his ass for you if it'll make you feel better." And then leaning close, he whispered conspiratorially, "Please say yes. Nothing would please us more than a chance to take big brother down a peg or two."

Sage felt nothing but relief when he saw Coral smile at Kip's nonsense. His youngest brother had such an uncanny ability to connect with women they'd accused him of being telepathic more than once. Standing, Kip shrugged. "Well, if we aren't going to get to pound on him, can we at least eat lunch? I'm starving."

Sage was grateful for the change of subject and from the smile lighting up Coral's face, he was sure she felt the same way. Lifting Coral in his arms, Sage settled her on the chair next to where he usually sat, grinning at the soft towel already covering her seat. He saw her puzzled look but didn't answer her unspoken question—*you'll see soon enough, beautiful girl.*

## Chapter Ten

LUNCH WAS A roller coaster ride unlike any Coral had ever experienced, from the disaster at the top of the stairs to Sage's heartfelt apology, to the wild stories the brothers shared about their childhood. But all of it had paled in comparison to the riot of emotions marching though her. God in heaven, her heart was about to beat right out of her chest. Before they'd settled down to eat, her stomach was doing somersaults, but it still managed to growl in agreement when Kip declared he was starving. "I can't help it, I'm a growing boy."

Coral was convinced Kip's flip response was more about distracting her than fact, but his brothers assured her with Kip, hunger was "situation normal." Sage had carried her to the table insisting she wasn't ready to walk yet, but she knew he was probably trying to minimize the stimulation to her clit. She had a news flash for him, just breathing was too much movement.

After setting her carefully on a chair covered with a soft towel, Sage leaned close speaking softly against her ear, "Spread your legs apart, pet. Hook your feet around the outside of the chair legs." When she followed his instructions she realized how exposed the position left her, the glass tabletop wasn't going to conceal anything from any of the brothers' view. She felt her face flush and knew she wasn't hiding her embarrassment. "Remember, we're all

Doms, pet. You're lovely and this is as good a time as any for you to become acquainted with one of the foundations of the lifestyle. As your Dom, it's my privilege and responsibility to push you to broaden your horizons. I'll always respect your hard limits, but be forewarned, pet—I'll challenge every "good girls don't" notion that pops into your pretty little head."

Coral wanted to argue she hadn't been given much moral guidance growing up, but the argument fell flat. She'd always prided herself on her ability to be honest with herself and she knew she'd managed to impose all those social restrictions on herself without any help from her parents. Sighing to herself, Coral accepted the fact hiding anything from Sage was going to be virtually impossible—*hell, he's going to see right through me...I'm thinking this could be a real pain in the ass—literally.* Keeping the protest to herself, Coral nodded in agreement even as she worried whether or not she'd ever be able to let go of her self-imposed rules.

Sage sat on her right and Colt took the chair on her left. When Sage's calloused palm slid up her thigh, she knew he was not only reminding her he considered her body his to play with, but he was sending a clear message to his brothers as well. Coral felt Colt's gaze on her, and when she turned she found him watching her closely "Which voice are you going to listen to, sweetness?" Coral sucked in a breath wondering for just second if perhaps she'd spoken out loud. "It's written all over your face, the turmoil between what your mind thinks is socially acceptable and what you know your body has been clamoring for as long as you can remember."

"How did you know?" All four of the brothers seated around the table chuckled and she felt her face flush with embarrassment—*again*.

"We aren't laughing at you Coral, we really aren't. We're laughing because it's a question submissives ask Doms all the time. The truth is we're trained to recognize subtle changes in your body language. But even more than that, we've had the benefit of each other's experience and that of our fellow club members," Phoenix's voice had a thread of steel she hadn't heard before—obviously there was a very real Dom lurking beneath his compassionate demeanor.

Surprisingly, it was Kip who did the most to allay her concerns. "Coral, always remember you have a safe word. If you start to get uncomfortable for heaven's sake, use yellow. A lot of the time a brief time-out is all you need, and it gives your Dom a heads up the situation is outpacing your ability to assimilate everything. And if you find yourself in over your head before you realize it's happening, call out red. You won't be penalized for using your safe word…unless it's clear you are doing it simply to manipulate a scene."

Coral took a deep breath and nodded. She was grateful for their reminders. It was easy to forget she had any control in this situation when she hadn't felt as though she had any real control in her life for a very long time. The rest of their lunch passed in a blur of conversation related to plans for the upcoming New Year's Eve party, mixed with updates on their various business interests. She was impressed at how involved Sage was in each of his brother's lives even though he didn't appear to micromanage them. Coral hadn't heard the door open and she was startled to see Brandt standing in the doorway.

Watching the Sheriff visually assess the situation sent a shiver of something between awareness and fear up her spine. Coral realized she was holding her breath awaiting his judgement, and she didn't take another breath until a smile tipped up the corners of his lips. It occurred to her she'd rarely seen Sheriff Brandt Morgan smile, but even this subtle show of amusement completely changed his appearance. *Holy hula-hipping hippos, how insanely good looking would he be if he actually smiled more often?* His deep voice brought her out of her musings, "Is this a punishment or a reward?"

Even though his question had been about her, Coral was sure it hadn't been directed at her, so she didn't respond. "Definitely a reward. And we were just on our way downstairs for a swim." Brandt's brows raised in surprised but he didn't seem willing to push the subject either.

"Before you take Coral downstairs to continue her…reward—I have a question for her." She could see his obvious hesitance to ask and she wondered what he could possibly consider so personal he didn't want to make the inquiry in front of his brothers. *Fuck a fat fairy, maybe he's decided you were involved with the drug dealer's death after all. He could send you back to Georgia in a heartbeat. If he doesn't believe you, there is no way in hell anyone else will. Fuck me, there are those blasted dots again.*

"Coral. Look at me. Now!" Sage's sharp command brought her attention to his face and she was surprised to see the concern in his eyes. "Jesus, you weren't breathing. Where on earth did you go?"

"I'm sorry, my imagination sort of ran away with me when I saw how hesitant Brandt was to ask me the question…"

Brandt shook his head, as he stepped forward. "No. It's nothing like that. I'm tired and frustrated because every damned lead I track down on those yo-yos who broke into your apartment nets absolutely nothing." Setting a small bag on the table Brandt spoke to Sage, "Here is the phone you asked me to pick up. We're keeping Coral's for a while longer. We know someone is tracking it so we've hidden it in her apartment and we're forwarding all the calls and messages to my phone." Returning his attention to her, he asked, "Who is Josie?"

Coral had just taken a drink of water and choked at the mention of her friend's name. *Damn, who knew you could actually choke on water?* "An old friend, why?" Her mind was scrambling, and she hadn't intended her response to sound as defensive as she knew it had. She'd always been fiercely protective of her friend's privacy—even before she became a worldwide musical phenomenon and old habits die-hard. Josie was better known as county music's newest superstar, Josephine Alta. But Josie hadn't always been the gorgeous woman fans worshipped today.

At one time Josie had been an awkward young girl who was bullied almost daily—that is until a new girl at their school intervened. Coral's childhood had been filled with bullies and she'd learned at an early age how to fight back, but what was even more important was she had also learned it was equally important to help those who couldn't help themselves. The day she'd stepped between Josie and the bullies, explaining to the posse of sixth grade bitches exactly how she'd rearrange their perky little faces, had been the last day they'd made Josie their target. It was also the day Coral and Josie became best friends.

Coral wasn't aware of how tightly she'd pulled her legs together until she felt Sage's fingers flex between her clenched thighs. Her hands were fisted in her lap, the cumulative effect was a punishing grip trapping Sage's hand against her sex. All five Morgan brothers' attention was focused on her, but to her relief they were looking at her face rather than the fact she'd reacted so negatively to Brandt's inquiry.

"Coral, your friend has texted you a couple of times. I've responded as you because it wasn't clear exactly who we were dealing with and for some reason we can't trace the number." Coral bit back her grin. *Yeah, I'll bet her people have made tracking her phone difficult at best.* "Now that I know the messages are from a friend I will forward them to you so you can respond personally. I'd suggest you do that fairly quickly as I believe your friend is beginning to get suspicious she isn't actually talking to you."

"I'm not surprised. She's usually pretty cautious." She turned to Sage who was already pulling the phone out of the bag Brandt handed him moments earlier.

"Don't suppose you'd be interested in elaborating on the *friend* comment?" She heard the concern in Sage's voice. *Damn it all to dented doorbells.* Sage had done so much for her she didn't want to give him any reason to doubt her.

Looking around the room, Coral realized if she was trusting these men with her life it seemed like a no-brainer they could be trusted with the truth about Josie. "I'm sorry. I wasn't trying to be overly secretive, I'm just accustomed to being really tight lipped about Josie. She'd been my best friend since we were kids, and even though our lives have taken very different paths, we've stayed in touch. The friend I know as Josie is actually Josephine Alta."

Sage's eyebrows notched up in surprise and she heard Colt's whistle from beside her. "Holy shit, Coral. That's awesome."

For once, Brandt was looking at her with an expression

that didn't make her think he was analyzing her. *Holy crap...did he actually just chuckle? As in almost amused?* "Well, that certainly explains why she was cautious—and why we couldn't get a bead on the phone. Hell, the NSA needs to hire her people."

After just a few texts, Coral realized how much she'd missed her friend during the past year. When she'd asked how Josie had gotten her phone number the response had been short and sweet, *"MONEY."* And while Coral was grateful her friend had tracked her down, it had also lead her to a disturbing conclusion. If Josie could find her, so could her ex, and Donny Sanders had more motivation than most people. By the time she'd finished texting with Josie, Coral's hands were shaking so badly she could barely hold the phone. Setting the small electronic device aside, she looked up to see all but one of the Morgan brothers visiting with one another. Sage's full attention was laser sharp and focused on her.

"YOU'RE WORRIED." HE hadn't needed to ask, he'd already known. "Pet, we already knew the phone you'd purchased was compromised. That sort of information is actually quite easy to obtain, and a star of Josephine's caliber would definitely have people who could get your number for her." Mixed emotions swirled in her eyes, but doubt wasn't one of them. Sage was both grateful and humbled by her trust.

"I guess I hadn't given enough thought to the fact they'd be waiting for me to get a phone." Running her fingers over the phone she'd just set down, he could almost hear the questions swirling through her mind. "What is to keep them from finding out about this one?"

The question had been whispered so softly, Sage might not have heard her if he hadn't been watching her so closely. "This phone is in my name, pet. The only people who would think to search for it that way are local." Looking up, Sage noted it had started to snow and decided to use the weather change as the distraction he thought Coral needed desperately. Threading his fingers through the soft curls framing her heart shaped face, he cupped his hand over her ear and used the position to turn her toward the windows lining the back of the house. "Look, pet. It's snowing. I can hardly wait to swim with you while the snow swirls a few feet away. Let's go, it's time for you to think about something else."

Sage watched Coral's eyes flit around the table in nervous anticipation. *Oh yeah. There is an exhibitionist deep inside my sweet sub—and I'm going to enjoy helping her explore that poorly kept secret.* There wasn't much he looked forward to more than helping Coral expand her sexual horizons. "Do you think you can make it down the steps on your own or would you like for me to remove the clit ring now?"

He loved the pink that stained her cheeks as she whispered, "Now? Right now?"

"Right now—right here." Sage was close enough he knew his warm breath had caressed the side of her face, even as she continued to stare out at the falling snow. He could almost hear her calculating the distance down to the pool. *Yes, sweetness it's* further *than the hallway upstairs that almost sent you into orbit. Reconsidering is a wise decision.*

"Can you do it without everyone seeing my pink bits?" This time she'd turned to face him and he was pleased to see the same mix of emotions he'd seen every time their topic of discussion had ventured to public displays.

Sage didn't even try to hold back his wicked grin, "Well, I suppose I could, but where would the fun be in that?"

Leading her down the stairs to the pool area several minutes later, Sage felt Coral begin to withdraw emotionally. He hoped the small scene they'd just done upstairs hadn't overwhelmed her too much—he wanted to push her, but knew there would be a fine line between enough and too much. Before they'd reached the large glass doors leading to the pool he turned her so she faced him. "Tell me what you're thinking, pet." He knew he'd surprised her and he hoped she'd blurt out her answer before taking time to edit it into something she thought he wanted to hear.

"I'm embarrassed about what I did just now...upstairs I mean. I can't believe I did that. How am I ever going to look your brothers in the face again? They have to think I'm beyond desperate. Geez, what was I thinking? I've never been like this before. And the worst part is I liked it. What does that even mean? I'm sure it isn't anything good." She was quickly working herself into a real *state* as his granny had always said. It needed to be shut down quickly before she got so caught up in her "good girl" limits she forgot about the pleasure she'd felt.

"Stop." His one word command had been sharp enough to snap her out of the downward spiral, but he could see the shame in her eyes and those unshed tears were almost enough to make him change the course he'd chosen. *No, stay the course with her. She needs your strength and guidance, not coddling.* "You didn't do anything wrong and if I hear you say it again I'll paddle your pretty little ass until I'm convinced you've gotten the message."

"You've spent entirely too much time trying to be good enough to make up for the shortcomings you saw in your parents. Not only were those efforts unnecessary then—damn, you were a child for God's sake. But now they're simply wasted energy because they're gone. Let them go and live your life, pet—you've earned it." The first tear to breach her lower lid and shimmer its way down her flushed cheek made his heart squeeze, but he was determined to hold himself back. If he gave in and cuddled her close she wouldn't understand how firmly he believed the words he'd just spoken. One of the things Sage had learned about submisives was they were usually far too caught up in doing what they felt was expected of them. Their need to please others trumped their own needs so frequently they forgot they deserved happiness as well.

With his hands on either side of her pretty face, Sage used his thumbs to brush away her tears. The tortured look of need in her eyes brought the Dom in him raging to the surface. "I'll help you, pet. You'll learn to see the deserving woman I see. And as for what happened upstairs—you showed my brothers how brave you are. Do you think they didn't know how far outside the lines you were coloring?" The grin that tipped up the corners of her deep pink lips let him know she was starting to relax once again. "I assure you your place in their hearts is even more solid now that they've seen first-hand how brave you are. Pet, the *willingness to try* is a magnetic pull no Dom can resist."

He suspected she was nearing the point of being completely overwhelmed. The day had been filled with distractions and while he had definitely wanted to switch her focus from the break-in, he didn't want to push her past her emotional limit either. "Let's swim. I think we could both use some time water time." For him swimming was a way to work out the kinks stress and physical labor left behind, he hoped she'd enjoy the pool as much as he did.

Stepping into the cavernous room he heard Coral's soft gasp. "I haven't actually been in this room yet. I just looked in from the door earlier. It's amazing—almost like a tropical jungle." She was right, the entire area was filled with tropical plants surrounding the pool as well as several sitting areas giving them each an illusion of privacy. The far end of the room was taken up with a fully functioning bar and grill. The kitchen behind the bar was capable of keeping even the largest party well fed. And God knew, the bar was well stocked enough to make every drink imaginable.

"The waterfall is my favorite feature. Come, let me show you." He grasped her hand and led her to the stone covered wall at the back of the pool. There were dressing rooms and showers behind the wall, but he'd insisted they leave a small area behind the falling water as a private area. He and his brothers had been young adults when his parents had decided to redo the basement adding the pool so they'd each had ideas of how to best use the new area in their romantic endeavors. Sage's dad still laughed about some of the outrageous and downright lurid suggestions they'd made. *Yeah, he laughed, but he damn well incorporated several of their ideas into the final design. The old saying about the fruit not falling far from the tree is truer than dad probably wants to admit.*

## Chapter Eleven

CORAL TRIED TO not let her mouth fall open like a fish out of water as she took in the sheer opulence of the Morgan's home, but damn the place was simply off the fucking chart amazing. She'd been bowled over by the upstairs and the master suite was bigger than the last house she'd shared with her mom and dad, but this? This was so much more than she'd expected…she could hardly take it all in. The entire space had obviously been designed for entertaining and Coral wondered if Sage brought all his women here—the thought was surprisingly depressing. She knew he was much more experienced, it wasn't as if she hadn't heard more than one story about the sexual prowess of the eldest Morgan brother from the local tongue waggers. But fantasizing about him and being faced with the reality of how he'd gotten all that experience were two very different things.

"What put that that frown on your face, sweetness?" *Oh course he wouldn't miss the change in your mood—what did you expect? The man doesn't miss much, that's for sure.*

Deciding to take a leap of faith, she blurted out her answer before good sense had a chance to kick in. "I wondered if you brought all of the women you…ummm, well…dated here. I know it isn't really any of my business, but it's what I was thinking about."

Coral felt her face flush with embarrassment but when

she tried to turn away, Sage stopped her. "No, pet. Look at me." When she met his gaze, Coral was surprised to see regret and a hint of embarrassment. "I'd love to tell you that you're the only woman I've ever brought into this part of the house, but I won't lie to you. But I can tell you it isn't a space I've shared often and I'm looking forward to making wonderful memories here with you."

WHAT SAGE DIDN'T mention was the fact Mackenzie was the only other woman he'd ever brought into this part of the house, and she'd spent the whole time complaining about how the humidity was destroying her newly styled hair. And God forbid he actually expected her to dip so much as a big toe in the *chlorinated* water. She'd gone on and on for hours about how horrible chemically treated water was for her sensitive skin. Hell, thinking back on their time together Sage wondered how he'd managed to ignore so many obvious signs they weren't right for one another.

Sage felt Coral's warm fingers stroking softly over his cheek, blinking down at her he realized he'd zoned out for a few seconds. "I'm sorry if I offended you. I shouldn't have said anything, I didn't mean to ruin the mood."

"No, pet. I'm glad you asked. I don't want there to be any secrets between us. I was just thinking about how dim witted I was with my ex, and how ungrateful I was when my brothers tried to point it out. Hell, Brandt and I were barely speaking by the time I pulled my head out of my ass and ended the relationship." He watched as something he didn't recognize passed over her expression. It had been so fleeting he wasn't even sure he hadn't imagined it, but it was gone quickly and he was ready to lose himself in Coral's sweet body so he let it go.

Stepping back, Sage crossed his arms over his chest and gave Coral a sinister smile. "Strip, pet." Hell, it shouldn't take long, he'd only let her put on a sundress—one quick pull over her head and she'd be naked as the day she was born, and he could hardly wait. When she glanced around the area he reached around her and gave her sweet ass a solid swat. "Your job is to follow instructions, pet. I'll worry about who is allowed to see what belongs to me." She surprised him when she nodded before quickly pulling the dress off. He wondered if she was afraid she might lose her courage if she waited too long. Taking a deep breath, Sage smiled. "God damn, you are fucking gorgeous. Your skin is flawless and the deep rose color your nipples turn when they peak is probably the prettiest color on the planet."

Leaning forward he circled his tongue around the delicate skin of her areola watching the tight bud of her nipple pull up even tighter. Throwing off his own clothes in record time, Sage watched the tip of Coral's tongue trace over her bottom lip, the look of hunger in her eyes unmistakable as her gaze dropped to his engorged cock. Hell, his dick must have known she was watching because it bounced happily against his lower abdomen—*damned thing is showing off for her.*

"I'm not a really good swimmer. I mean, I won't drown or anything, but I'm not an expert." She might have been talking about swimming, but he wasn't entirely convinced her words didn't hold a deeper meaning.

"Not to worry, I'll be happy to help you—*always*. Remember that, pet, because it's important. Anything you need, you only have to ask, if I don't know the answer we'll find it together." When he saw her nod in understanding, he grinned before scooping her up in his arms and walking down the sloping concrete into the warm water. "Our dad insisted the pool have a zero entry feature because he said someday he would be too old to do cannonballs off the top of the waterfall." Coral laughed, as he'd hoped she would—it was definitely time to lighten the mood. "You think I'm kidding, but I'm forewarning you, he is a demon with cannonballs. He'll soak you if he gets half a chance."

They swam and played for several minutes before Coral noticed Colt leaning against the corner of the stone structure housing the waterfall. There were stairs hidden behind a small outcropping of rock letting the more adventurous swimmers a chance to use the platform as a diving board. Sage had invited his brother to join them contingent upon Coral's agreement. His brother had shed his shirt and shoes, but he'd left his low riding jeans in place. Sage watched Coral's eyes dilate as she took in Colt's appearance, and he wondered if she was going to be brave enough to admit how interested she was in a ménage scene.

When he'd researched the books on Coral's e-reader, he had been surprised to find so many selections featuring polyamorous relationships. He looked forward to introducing her to Tobi West. The lovely spitfire who'd married Kent and Kyle West would be a perfect sounding board for Coral. Mama Morgan and Lilly West were first cousins, but had grown up together and considered themselves closer than most sisters. The boys had spent time together during school holidays and vacations so Sage hadn't hesitated to call the West brothers and ask for a favor. They'd laughed at his suggestion Tobi would be a good role model for

Coral, but they'd agreed to set up a time for the two women to speak privately in a Facetime call.

"Cousin, I'm not sure you know exactly what you're getting in to." Kent's teasing words bounced through Sage's mind as he watched Coral pull her bottom lip between her teeth, nibbling on it—a nervous habit he'd noticed she fell into whenever she started to feel overwhelmed.

Kyle had shaken his head and smiled. "God only knows what Tobi might say, I've given up trying to predict what she'll do in any given situation. But knowing this will be important to our mom will make a huge difference, she might actually behave."

"Oh yeah, those two are thick as thieves."

"And about as trustworthy when they're together." Kyle's grin gave away his amusement, and despite his obvious sarcasm, Sage had seen the amusement dancing in his eyes. They'd set up a time during the upcoming week and the two former SEALs agreed to call Brandt to see if they could help with the investigation. *Like those two and their merry band of former Special Forces operatives don't have resources the rest of us can only dream of.* "We aren't as limited by legalities as Brandt is—perhaps we can lend a hand."

Watching Coral's respiration rate kick up and her eyes dilate as she watched Colt move closer, his bare feet silent on the concrete pool deck, Sage could see the fluidity in his brother's movements, something their mother always claimed was due in part to Colt's innate musical talent. Their mom had always sworn Colt's athletic ability and grace during bull rides was because he simply moved to the music he'd always claimed to hear in his head. Sage had teased his brother about it when they were kids, but as they'd grown up he'd learned to appreciate Colt's musical skill—God knew he hadn't gotten that particular genetic gift.

Stepping forward, Sage blocked her view of Colt standing at the edge of the pool. Lifting her chin with his fingers, he watched a pink flush move over her cheeks. "Pet, nothing happens that you aren't comfortable with. You seem to have an interest in ménage and Colt has agreed to help us explore it—but he and I are both adamant about this being your decision." They'd discussed shared scenes briefly, but they hadn't discussed specifics. Sage had emphasized the fact he would never be interested in sharing her permanently, but he'd asked her to consider ménage scenes. Now, watching her worried expression, he wondered if he hadn't pushed ahead too quickly.

"I would like to try, but I'm worried you'll..." when she wasn't able to finish, Sage was fairly certain he knew what direction she'd been heading.

"You're worried I'll become jealous? Or perhaps I will think less of you because you let another man touch you—even though I've set this in motion?" She didn't even have to answer, he saw the truth in her eyes.

"Yes. I'm afraid I'll ruin everything."

"Baby, a huge part of a Dom's job is to help his or her submissive explore their interests. But, even then, I'd never do anything I thought would come between the two of us—because at the end of the day, your happiness is all that matters to me." He gave her a few seconds to process what he'd said before continuing. Sage enjoyed sharing a woman because it was easy to miss subtle shifts in body language when you were caught up in the moment, and there was no doubt he lost his mind the minute his cock slid into Coral's sweet heat. "There won't be any jealousy between us—ever. I assure you, Colt knows exactly what is expected and even though he'll be taking cues from you, ultimately he'll be taking instructions from me. I'll still be in charge of your pleasure—because you belong to me, pet."

Sage was thrilled to see the Coral's shoulders relax and the spark of interest light her eyes. He didn't think she realized he'd slowly turned her so Colt was now able to see her reactions, it would give him an idea of how to begin. *Information is always power in D/s scenes, but it's critical with newbies.* When she nodded her head, he shook his own and suddenly her face was filled with worry that she'd made some sort of mistake.

"You need to speak the words, sweetness. It's important we are both completely clear on your agreement. I'm not going to lie, I hope like hell you agree because you are amazing. But remember, I'm here to strengthen your bond with Sage, not to replace it. This is all about your pleasure, baby." Amazing wasn't really accurate, the truth was Sage had found a remarkable woman, and Colt couldn't wait to see how she'd blossom once the danger to her was taken care of. It was easy to see she craved the sense of belonging she'd find in their family, they just needed to convince her there were various roles to choose from.

As soon as she whispered, "Yes. I'd like to try." Colt started pealing his softly faded Levis down his legs. They'd already been unsnapped and damn if he hadn't enjoyed watching her pretty green eyes moving over his bare chest to focus on the gap at the top of his jeans. Colt never professed to having been a saint during his years on the rodeo circuit. He and his friends had elevated fucking beautiful women to an art form for more years than he cared to remember, but he already knew it wouldn't be the way he'd be getting relief this afternoon.

Sage had been quite clear, his "nobody slides into her pussy but me" declaration hadn't surprised Colt. Sage could be a possessive bastard when found something he really wanted, and there wasn't any doubt this woman was exactly what the eldest Morgan brother wanted. They'd all known she belonged to Sage from the first day he'd told them about her. The disaster with Mackenzie had shaken Sage's confidence, the worst of it being how he'd begun questioning his ability to judge people. Colt was thrilled to see the spark of self-assurance and purpose in his brother's eyes again.

Walking into the pool, Colt looked up at his brother and grinned. "Have you taken her behind the falls yet?"

"No. I waited." Colt heard the implied *for you* but he doubted Coral had.

Standing in front of Coral, he could almost hear the wheels of her mind spinning wildly as she tried to figure out exactly what she was supposed to say and do. Pressing a chaste kiss to the center of her forehead he whispered, "Don't overthink this, sweetness. We'll take care of everything. It's one of the joys of being a submissive—all you need to do is enjoy the pleasure and follow instructions. No need to worry endlessly about what you should be saying or doing." Colt loved the look of relief he saw in her soft green eyes. Taking her hand in his he turned her toward the open area of the pool. "Come on, swim with me."

## Chapter Twelve

CORAL WAS HAVING such a great time swimming with Sage and Colt she'd almost forgotten the fact she was naked—*how on earth did that happen?* She'd rarely gone swimming as a kid, her parents had considered it a waste of money. The few times she'd gone she'd been forced to wear something she'd picked up at a second-hand store. Just remembering how *creepy* she'd felt wearing someone else's swimsuit made her want to shudder. She could feel the sexual tension growing between the three of them, but she was taking Colt's advice and letting them set the pace. There was definitely something to be said about not worrying over all the details of social niceties. After struggling for so long to survive day-to-day, Coral was surprised how relieved she felt to let someone else shoulder the responsibility...even if it was only for the afternoon.

Colt's fingers brushing along the side of her face brought Coral back to the moment. Startled, she looked around and was surprised to find Sage missing. "What put that look of sadness in your eyes, sweetness?"

"I'm sorry. I was thinking about how nice it felt to not have to worry about anything for a while and it reminded me how temporary this might be." Taking a deep breath she decided to take a leap of faith and trust Colt with one of her greatest fears. "I'm worried I'll have to leave. I'm not sure I could live with myself if something happened to Sage or one of you because of me." Coral felt her entire body react—just the thought made her almost ill. Looking around, she felt her voice crack when she asked, "Where's Sage?"

Colt didn't hesitate, he wrapped her in his arms. Coral was shocked and knew her spine had gone ramrod straight, but when Colt simply held her close, she slowly began to relax. "Sage wanted us to spend a few minutes alone while he sets up something special for you." He leaned back pressing kisses to both cheeks. "You're not going anywhere, sweetness. We're going to teach you all about how families are supposed to work. We all understand your concerns but we also we have the advantage of knowing adversity actually makes us stronger. What you haven't experienced is strength in numbers, but I promise you it's a lesson we're going to love teaching you. And you need to remember who you're dealing with, sweetness."

He'd obviously seen the question in her face because he chuckled. "Baby girl you wear your heart on your sleeve. And thank God for small favors, because even though we're all Doms, we're still men and sometimes the inner workings of a woman's mind can baffle even the most astute men on the planet." He gave her a quick hug before leading her to one of the benches built into the side of the pool. Sitting down beside her, he explained, "Sage is a problem solver—he always has been. I swear he would have been the one to take over for dad even if he hadn't been the oldest and led in that direction from day one."

She understood that he was really telling her Sage would *fix* this for her, what she couldn't help but wonder was *at what cost*? "As for me," Colt continued, "I spent the better part of two decades riding on the backs of two thousand pounds of pissed off bulls who not only wanted to buck me off, they wanted to steamroll me once I hit the ground. Sorry if I don't seem terrified of some two bit drug dealer who wasn't smart enough to know what a treasure he had." Tapping her on the tip of her nose to emphasize the fact he'd been talking about her, Coral could feel her cheeks flush with embarrassment.

"Now we've come to the family bad-ass. Brandt's years as a Navy SEAL didn't leave him without any skills, sweetness. And just in case you wondered, nobody uses our home gym more than Brandt—hell, I'll bet you he is in as good or better physical condition now as he ever was during his time in the Special Forces. The man is lightning fast and fiercely protective of the people he cares about." Coral knew everything Colt had said was true, but what she alone seemed to know was Brandt Morgan not only didn't trust her, he didn't even seem to like her.

"Now, Phoenix is insanely smart—hell, he was accepted into Mensa before he was old enough to drive, and on a ranch that's saying a lot since we all learned to drive long before the great state of Montana thought we should." She was surprised to see a tinge of pink on his cheeks, when she bumped her shoulder against his to show she understood the message, he laughed. "Hell, Sage and I used to tease Phoenix and Kip they weren't taught to drive until middle school because they were dim-witted, but honestly with three older boys it just wasn't necessary." He shook his head as if it would bring his thoughts back in focus and strange as it seemed, that action endeared him to her even more. "Anyway, Phoenix is not someone your ass-hat ex wants as an enemy. With the limited information he was given about Sanders, I can promise you the man is already suffering the consequences. His credit has likely been destroyed, he won't be able to rent or buy anything. I'm sure he's suddenly found himself *persona no grata* at all his usual haunts because little brother would have scoured his credit card and bank history to find all his favorite hangouts." When he turned to her, his expression was almost evil. "In short, it sucks to be him."

Coral giggled, "I know this probably makes me a terrible person, but I can't tell you how happy it makes me to hear this." The mocking look of shock on his face made her laugh. "It's one thing to meet violence with violence, but knowing he's already being held accountable makes me want to jump up and down clapping my hands like a three year old."

Colt's eyes narrowed slightly, their usual deep green going impossibly darker. "Oh baby, I'd love to see you jumping up and down. Not only would be I love to see you that happy, but seeing those beautiful breasts bouncing would be enough to make a grown man weep." His words sent a flood of desire racing through her so hot it made her gasp. When his gaze lowered to her breasts Coral felt her nipples draw up into tight peaks—hell, you'd think he'd actually touched her.

Clearing her thought, Coral ducked her head trying to sort through her conflicting emotions. How could she be so attracted to Sage's brother? Did it make her disloyal? Trying to bring the conversation back to a place she felt more comfortable, Coral asked, "What about Kip?" The knowing grin Colt gave her let Coral know her attempt to change the subject hadn't gone unnoticed.

"Everyone thinks Kip is a goof-off who doesn't care about anything but his next sexual conquest, but I think there is a lot more to Kip than what is on the surface. There is a reason women love Kip—he understands them better than most men because he has the ability to hear what people aren't saying." As strange as Colt's words might have sounded, Coral understood exactly what he meant. Pointing toward the waterfall, Colt grinned. "As much as I've enjoyed our chat, I'm looking forward to seeing how you like the surprise Sage has for you. Let's go." Pulling her back into the deeper water, Colt led her to where the water fell from the rock ledge above. "It's easier if you swim through under the water, come on."

Coral barely had time to gulp in a breath before Colt pulled her under. She followed him under the pounding water and was surprised to see an open area with twinkling lights along the sides of the pool. The water was also considerably warmer and she'd no sooner surfaced when the water started to bubble around her. "Oh my God, a hot tub? Really? Oh, I've died and gone to heaven."

When she looked up she was surprised to see Sage leaning against the rock wall smiling at her. There was a small table with what looked like a bottle of champagne, glasses, and a bowl of strawberries. There were two lounge chairs to the side and she noticed what looked like a black leather duffle bag on the floor beside one of the chairs. But the thing that really caught her attention was the look of hunger in Sage's eyes. Even though the lighting was subdued, there was no way be mistake the look on his face. He didn't say anything, he simply held out his hand and without even thinking about it, Coral swam to him.

As she walked up the narrow steps out of the water, Sage wrapped her in a warm bath sheet. Colt was already filling the champagne flutes, and grinning at her as he popped a whole strawberry into his mouth. The sexual energy surrounding them was almost crackling and Coral felt her body responding before either of them had a chance to actually touch her. Pulling the towel from her, Sage tossed it to the side and pulled her against his chest. "Tell me the safe word system we established, pet."

By the time she'd finished reciting what she'd learned, Coral could have sworn every single cell in her body was vibrating with the need to be touched. When she shivered Colt grinned. "Cold, sweetness?" He nodded in understanding when she shook her head, but he didn't say anything else.

There was something different about Sage, almost as if he'd been infused with a new sense of purpose and Coral instinctively knew she was about to see the sexual Dominant side of Sage in a whole new light. When she'd finished her champagne, Sage took the glass from her hand and set it aside. "I'm going to ask you one more time, pet—are you ready to play?"

Coral had read enough about BDSM scenes to recognize the start of a scene and she knew it was time to either put a halt to things or plunge ahead. Looking from one man to the other, Coral couldn't imagine making any other decision. Nodding her head, she answered, "Yes, Sir." She could have sworn she heard them both growl, but the thought was quickly eclipsed by the scorching kiss Sage gave her. His tongue traced the line of her lips before pushing in what only could be described as a plundering claim of her mouth. Coral felt more than heard the moan of need that rose up from the deepest part of her soul. By the time he pulled back, Coral's head was spinning and she felt her body lean toward his, subconsciously seeking his touch.

"Let's get your punishment out of the way." *What? Punishment?*

Colt's chuckle drew her attention. "You didn't think

he'd forget the orgasm you had at the top of the stairs did you?" Coral couldn't find the words to answer, she just stood there gapping at them trying to make sense of it all. "Come on, let's get you into position because I can hardly wait to play and this punishment is the only thing standing in my way." Before Coral could voice any of the questions rocketing through her head, she found herself bent at the waist grasping the edge of a chaise lounge. Colt pushed her feet further apart, and then instructed her to flatten her back. *Sure...let's make sure all my pink bits are hanging out there for everyone to see.*

The first slap of Sage's hand rocked her up on her tiptoes, her gasp changing to a soft groan as heat replaced the sting. The swat surprised her, but the part that stunned her was how quickly the pain morphed into something entirely different. The first slap was followed quickly by another four, each marking a different spot. Coral felt her pussy flooding with moisture and she sent up a silent prayer they wouldn't notice how her traitorous body was responding—but that pipe dream vanished when she felt calloused fingers sliding through the slick petals of her pussy. Colt helped her stand up, and she was grateful for his support when everything around her started to spin. Turning her to face Sage, Colt whispered against her ear, "Look at your Master, sweetness. Look at how much he's enjoying the sweet syrup you didn't think he knew about."

*Holy humiliation!* She wished the floor would open up and swallow her whole. "Fuck me, you respond so perfectly I don't even know where to start—I want it all and I want it right now. It nearly killed me to finish that punishment when I could smell your arousal, pet. And, watching you lift your perfect ass seeking the next slap of my hand was almost enough to send me over the edge." *What? Oh happy hamsters, please tell me I didn't really do that.*

MACKENZIE STARED AT the screen of the larger of her two laptops, listening as Donny Sanders gave her excuse after excuse for not meeting her in person as they'd originally planned. How the slut from the hardware store had gone from dating this idiot to Sage Morgan amazed her. "Hey, somebody is fucking with my bank and credit cards. Nothing works and I'm waiting on someone to wire me some damned money." Mackenzie fought to keep from rolling her eyes, obviously the man hadn't done any research into the men his ex was staying with. She'd bet her last nickel she knew exactly who was behind the man's financial woes, but at this point she felt he hadn't earned any more of her help. If he wasn't smart enough to check out the men he'd be going up against, it wasn't really her problem.

She'd already made plans to attend the Morgan's party tomorrow night, it shouldn't be that difficult to drive a wedge between a woman as plain as Coral Williams and a man as socially prominent as Sage Morgan. Mac still seethed every time she thought back on the trouble Brandt Morgan had caused her. Maybe she'd arrange a case of mistaken identity for the moron babbling on about his misfortune.

Deciding she'd heard enough, Mackenzie tapped out a message on her second laptop before attaching a picture of Brandt Morgan and sending it to Mr. Excuses. "I've got to go, but I've sent you a picture of the man you need to deal with if you want to get to your little eye-witness. I'll be in touch." With that she disconnected the call and leaned back, letting the soft leather of her suite's office chair wrap around her shoulders. She was using the last of her inheritance to fund this trip, but in the end it would definitely be worth the investment. The Morgans were worth millions and she fully intended to attach herself to each and every one of those precious dollars. Grabbing her purse, Mackenzie headed to the door. Her spa appointment was another investment in her future—the only way to win a war was to bring everything you had to the battle. *Little Miss Plain Jane won't have a snowball's chance in hell of keeping Sage after tomorrow night.*

## Chapter Thirteen

IF SAGE HADN'T been so close to losing control he might have found Coral's embarrassment amusing, instead those pink cheeks were more like tossing gas on a fire. The hot flare of need racing up his spine had him signaling Colt to raise the chaise and get into position. To Sage's surprise, his brother pulled Coral into his arms, holding her close for several seconds before threading his fingers through her long hair and tilting her face up to his. "Sweetness, I can't think of a single thing in the world I want more than to slide between these pretty lips." Colt's fingertip traced over Coral's lips in a slow stroke and Sage watched as she shuddered in response. *Damn, little brother has learned some new moves since we last shared a woman.*

Colt hadn't liked Mackenzie and had flat out refused to touch her during the time Sage had dated her. Hell, Kip had been the only one of his brothers willing to share a scene with them and Mackenzie had scoffed at the idea. She'd laughed in Kip's face citing his age as reason enough to reject him, Sage had been infuriated, but the guiding tenants of the BDSM lifestyle dictated if one partner was opposed then it was off the table. Sage gave more than lip service to safe, sane, and consensual, the words were the centerpiece of the commitment he'd made to every submissive he'd ever played with, and as angry as he'd been at her for hurting Kip's feelings, he'd known it was as far as the discussion was going to go.

"But I want to give you one more chance to back out of this, because once you touch me, I'm fairly certain I'm going to have the same look of desperation I saw in big brother's eyes a moment ago." Colt's words brought Sage back to the moment, and he watched Coral's eyes go wide. A split second later she stood up on her tip toes pressing her lips against Colt's in a kiss Sage was sure she'd intended to be short and sweet. *She's in for a big surprise.* Colt loved kissing women. Hell, every woman Sage knew swore Colt Morgan had a PhD in kissing. Sage grinned when his brother growled and tightened his fingers in Coral's hair as he took control of the kiss.

Returning his attention to his toy bag, Sage pulled out what he needed, setting everything on the small table between the chairs. Colt ended the kiss with a sigh before turning Coral to face him again while he moved into place. Sage looked down at Coral, and struggled to hold back his grin. Damn, her nipples were almost tight enough already for the clamps he'd chosen and Colt hadn't done anything but kiss her—*show off.* Grasping the buds between his fingers, Sage rolled them as he pinched each nub with just enough pressure to make her moan. When he knelt in front of her, pulling first one and then the other into his mouth he was pleased to feel her arching her back and pressing the sweet berries even further between his lips. He obliged by pressing the tender nub against the roof of his mouth, and was rewarded with her soft plea for more.

Slipping the small circle clamps into place, Sage adjusted them until he saw her eyes widen and heard her breath catch. *Perfect.* He wasn't a sadist, the goal wasn't pain for pain's sake. Sage merely wanted to enhance the feeling of her movements while she leaned over Colt, he hoped the distraction was enough to make the rest of his plan easier to execute. *Execute? Christ, I have to get my head out of the boardroom and into the bedroom or I'm going to fuck this up.* Realizing he could ruin things with Coral if he didn't keep his head in the game brought him up short.

Sage had never *failed* at anything—and he damned well didn't plan to start now. As the firstborn he'd never lacked for parental attention, school had been a cakewalk, attracting the attention of members of the opposite sex had also been easy, and he'd never struggled financially. Realizing how easy his life had been compared to Coral's was humbling indeed. Vowing to find some way to enrich her life every single day, Sage reached forward to flick the small diamonds swinging from the gold chains of her nipple clamps. "So pretty. I love the way the light catches on each of the stone's facets sending sparkles of light dancing over your beautiful skin." Using the edge of his fingernail, Sage traced a line connecting several of the glimmering dots and smiled when goose bumps raced over the surface.

"You are so beautiful, pet—you take my breath away. But the beauty on the outside is just the tip of the iceberg. It's your strength of character shining through that tells the tale. And your interest in the lifestyle? Oh, baby—that is just icing on a very sweet cake." He could see her preparing to respond, but when she took a deep breath the diamonds were set into motion once again. Sage grinned when her eyes glazed over and he saw her knees wobble. Moving her in to position, he watched as Coral's eyes went impossibly wide when she realized she was kneeling directly in front of Colt's very eager cock.

"I TOLD YOU I could hardly wait to feel those luscious lips wrapped around my cock, sweetness." Colt drew her focus to his face with his fingers, and she felt her face heat with embarrassment. *Just shoot me now—nothing like being caught ogling a guy's goods.* "Oh don't be shy, I love seeing that look of longing in your eyes, sweetness. Spread your knees further apart, and I want to feel that pretty pink tongue licking the head before you blow my mind."

Coral's hands were trembling when she placed them on Colt's thighs, steadying herself as she moved her knees further apart. His hand covered hers, his voice softer than it had been a few seconds earlier, "My brother is a lucky man and I'm damned grateful to be a part of this scene. Remember, the only thing we're expecting of you is your surrender. Give yourself over to the feelings and follow the instructions we give you. I promise you every one of those directives will be with your pleasure in mind."

Coral felt herself relax, she appreciated Colt taking the time to calm her rioting nerves, because she knew it would make it much easier for her to enjoy their time together. Looking up at Sage, she saw him leaning against the wall with his arms crossed over his chest and his ankles crossed in a pose she suspected was deceptively casual. She could tell he'd placed items on the small table but damn if he hadn't covered them with a small towel. Coral frowned and both men chuckled. "Pet, you didn't think it was going to be that easy did you? Doms are by nature sneaky, it's a necessary part of our continual effort to stay in control—just part of the package, pet."

"A word to the wise, sweetness—you might want to check those frowns because they'll usually get you a swat or two." Coral returned her gaze to Colt, being careful to blank her expression. "No, sweetness, your Master isn't going to want to see the emotional distance either. But I can promise you, he won't like seeing you frown when something hasn't gone your way. Doms take it as a small sign you don't trust them to provide you with what you need." On one level Coral understood what Colt was trying to tell her...but on the other hand, she had no clue how to control her reactions.

Pushing her concerns aside, she decided to focus on what she did know. Wrapping her hand around Colt's cock, Coral wasn't surprised to find her fingers didn't meet. When she ran her tongue around the rim she was shocked to find how different he and Sage tasted. Holding back her giggle, Coral wondered how her life could have changed so much in such a short period of time. In just a couple of days, she'd gone from living alone in a tiny apartment to sharing a home larger than any she'd ever seen with five men. Coral hadn't ever professed to understand the mysterious workings of fate, and she wasn't going to waste this time trying to sort it out. Letting herself fall into the moment sounded like a much more enjoyable place for her to go.

As soon as she surrendered herself completely to the experience, simply enjoying how Colt felt sliding between her lips, the way his hips involuntarily jerked in response to her tongue tracing the small V along the bottom of his corona. The stones on the nipple clamps tugged every time she moved sending pleasure skittering down her spine and straight into her core.

No sooner had she taken Colt into her mouth, then she felt Sage's hand slide from her ass to the base of her skull. She stilled as he spoke against her ear, "Watching you chip away at Colt's control is one of the hottest things I've ever seen."

The warmth of Sage's breath against the shell of her ear made her groan, which in turn elicited some very creative cursing from Colt. "Jesus, Joseph, and Mother Mary, have mercy. Big brother, unless you want this to be over in about a half a second you better distract your darling sub because she has a devil-blessed mouth. Holy hell, at this rate she is going to destroy me in T-minus sixty seconds."

She heard Sage's laughter before she felt he move behind her, "Well, let's see if we can't distract her a bit. Pet, I'm looking forward to claiming every part of you, but before I can enjoy this lovely little piece of heaven, you need to be properly prepared." When his finger rimmed the outer ring of her rear hole, Coral gasped and felt herself clench against the touch. A stinging slap was followed by a drizzle of something cool. "Don't try to keep me out, pet. You belong to me—that means every part of you is mine to claim. Short of using your safe word, you are not the one in charge." As strange as it sounded—even in her own mind, Coral felt something in her let go and she was delighted with the lightness that filled her heart.

SLIDING HIS LITTLE finger into Coral's tight ass was going to go down as one of the most erotic moments of Sage's life. After one swat and a curt reminder that she belonged to him, the amazing woman pressing back into his touch had given herself over to him completely. He'd wanted nothing more than to throw her over his shoulder and spring back upstairs to the master suite with her. But this was whole scene had been planned to give Coral the opportunity to explore a small piece of the lifestyle, and he wasn't going to deny her this opportunity.

He planned to ask her a very important question tomorrow night during the party, and she needed to know as much about his life as possible if she was going to make a decision about sharing it. What might have looked like a sudden decision to an outsider had actually come on the heels of months of getting to know the woman he'd found such comfort holding close last night. Wrapping her in his arms, knowing she felt safe enough to fall asleep in his embrace had touched his soul. Sage had heard the moment the nightmare started to pull her under. But his touch and soothing words had settled her quickly, and the whole thing was over almost as quickly as it started. Knowing she trusted him on a subconscious level was gift straight from the heavens—there wasn't anything he wouldn't do for this woman.

Colt's rasped, "You need to step up to the plate, big brother, because I can't hold on forever." Sage understood exactly what his brother was saying because he'd been on the receiving end of Coral's oral focus this morning in the shower. The look of adoration in Coral's eyes as she'd knelt in front of him, water streaming down the sides of her pretty face had snapped the last thread of his control. He didn't want this to end too soon so it was time to change his direction.

Sage pulled his fingers back, then carefully slid the small plug he'd gotten for her into place. It wasn't much larger than the two fingers he'd used to stretch her sensitive tissues so he knew the burn would have been minimal despite the gasp he'd heard her make around Colt. "We're going to start small and work up slowly, pet. I don't want to damage these tender tissues." As an experienced sexual Dominant, Sage had seen the aftermath of anal sex scenes gone bad, and it hadn't been pretty. He couldn't imagine subjecting Coral to anything so painful, and he would definitely be taking all the time needed to make sure she was ready before claiming the last bit of her sexuality.

Colt gave him a look that shouted, "Stop yammering and start fucking." Sage wanted to laugh out loud because his next youngest brother was renowned for his ability to hold off his own release. He'd seen submissives clamor for Colt's attention when they'd visited their favorite kink clubs, and even though he hadn't been to the club since he'd met Coral. Sage doubted anything had changed.

Pressing the head of his cock against her entrance, the heat from her core wrapped him in pleasure, Sage fought the urge to push in balls deep in one long thrust. "You're so hot, pet. And it's an invitation I can't resist. You're going to feel impossibly tight with the little plug in your ass—are you ready to fly with me?" Sage didn't wait for her to reply, he was taking her with him no matter what.

"Please. Now. Need," Coral's gasped words sounded as desperate as Sage felt.

"Let's see who goes over first, you or Colt." Sage had gotten a glimpse of Coral's competitive spirit during last summer's festival activities. There's nothing like a good old-fashioned three-legged race to bring out someone's inner Olympian. He was gaining ground in small thrusts, slowly stretching her to accommodate his girth, but damn if she wasn't scorching him with her heat. There was a very real chance his control was going to snap in record time and he was determined not to be the only one tumbling end over end into bliss.

"I don't know what your plan is big brother, but I suggest you kick it up a notch or twelve. Because we're about a half a shake from a championship ride here," Colt's thinly veiled reference to an eight-second finish line wasn't lost on Sage. Now that he'd managed to fully seat himself inside Coral he was reluctant to move, but duty called.

"As much as I love being so deep inside you I can feel your heart beating, I do love feeling your pussy rippling around me during those seconds before you lose yourself in release. And the feel of your muscles clamping down on me like a vice? The sweetest torture I've ever known." Picking up his pace Sage wanted to shout for joy when Coral's muscles immediately started rippling around him.

"Sweetness you are about to get a taste of me, if you don't want it, you need to let go—right fucking now." Sage could see the Coral's back muscles flex and knew she wasn't going to let go. *That's my girl.*

Leaning over her, he changed the angle so the stiff ridge around the head of his cock hit her G-spot with each thrust. Sage wrapped one arm around Coral's waist because one of the things he'd learned about his sweet sub was how quickly her muscles became liquid once her orgasm was over. With the other hand he circled the sweet little bundle of nerves he could feel poking out seeking his attention. And attention it was going to get. Using the juices of Coral's arousal to coat his fingers, Sage circled the small bundle of nerves several times enjoying the way her hips bucked beneath him in response.

Biting down gently on the tender spot where her shoulder and neck joined, Sage recognized the significance of his action. There was something purely primitive about the act, and rather than being embarrassed, Sage found an unreasonable amount of pride in the small act. It wasn't about the mark he could barely see, it was how she'd reacted. Sage knew she was in the deep end of her orgasm, but she was still gulping down Colt's release as her entire body convulsed beneath him. And the clamp of her inner muscles around his cock stole the last shred of his control. Shouting her name, he emptied himself in her, and hoped like hell he'd be able to hold her up when he was barely staying on his feet.

Rolling her on to the lower chaise, Sage cuddled her on his lap leaving his brother gasping on the higher lounger. "Christ, I think she stole a piece of my soul, brother." Sage watched a small smile paint her expression, as a pink flush moved over her cheeks.

"You are truly amazing, pet. And I can't tell you how proud I am of how well you handled that scene." And calling it a scene was a huge understatement considering Coral had just sealed her fate—she was his, and he didn't care what it took to convince her.

## Chapter Fourteen

CORAL COULDN'T HOLD back her tears of relief when Sage's sweet mama showed up early the next afternoon, her arms laden with packages. How Patsy Morgan had managed to find the perfect dress and matching shoes in her size on such short notice was a mystery to Coral. But, she was humbled and grateful beyond measure by the Morgan matriarch's gesture. The only bump in the road had come when Coral had promised to repay her. Patsy had pulled back as if she'd been slapped and Coral could have sworn she heard all six men in the room gasp collectively.

Blinking at everyone's shocked expressions, Coral tried to explain. "But it would be wrong for me to expect you to just buy me an outfit." Coral had been equally shocked the other woman thought she would be so presumptuous.

Patsy wasn't much taller than Coral and God knew she didn't look old enough to have raised five grown sons, but Coral found out very quickly Patsy Morgan was pure steel forged by fire on the inside. "Now you listen to me young lady. It is my right and privilege to spend Dean's money any way I see fit." She waved her hand in a semi-circle around them. "You see all these boys? *Boys!* It's all the man would ever give me, so he owes me a lot more than just getting to buy a pretty dress and a pair of shoes for my son's girl. Now, you get yourself upstairs and get ready because I'm just dying to see how it looks on you."

Patsy might have sounded indignant, but there was nothing but warmth in her eyes as she'd regarded Coral. This was a woman who didn't hesitate to stand up for those she loved. Coral was sure the mama bear analogy had started because of women like the one standing in front of her.

It had been so long since anyone other than Charlotte had shown her anything vaguely resembling motherly concern. Coral thought her heart might burst she was so moved by the gesture. There were times when she missed her own mother so much the pain felt like it hadn't faded at all. Coral didn't even try to hold back the tears as she gave Patsy a bruising hug before hurrying up the stairs. If she'd stayed downstairs, she knew she was going to end up blubbering like an idiot in front of the whole clan.

Two hours later, standing in front of the pedestal mirror in the master suite, Coral marveled at how perfectly everything fit her. She'd never had a dress with any kind of embellishment, always assuming they would draw unwanted attention. Coral was grateful Patsy had forced her to be brave. What would it have been like to grow up with a mother who encouraged her to try new things? To have siblings who backed you whether they agreed with your decision or not? How could she even consider walking away from Pine Creek and the Morgans?

Coral was almost giddy watching the gold threads woven into random patterns of the black fabric shimmer as they reflected even the smallest bits of light. The effect wasn't glaring—it didn't shout *look at me, look at me*. The soft glimmers would subtly catch the eye but wouldn't make her the center of attention—and that was perfect. The shoes had moderate heels—nothing sky high, thank

God, because Coral had never mastered the art of walking gracefully in heels. Pivoting first one foot and then the other, she couldn't help feeling like Cinderella before the ball. The big difference was...this outfit had been assembled by a woman whose capacity for love seemed capable of expanding at will rather than a fairy Godmother whose magic would evaporate at the stroke of midnight.

Sage knew Coral hadn't heard him enter the master suite, and he took advantage of the opportunity to observe her unobtrusively for a few moments. There wasn't a doubt in his mind these stolen seconds would burn themselves into his memory for all eternity. *God, she glows from the inside out.* According to his brothers he'd wasted far too much time making his move on the sweet woman standing in front of him. Maybe he had moved at a snail's pace, but he damned well wasn't going to waste another day. He wasn't going to let anything stand in his way tonight—he was going to seal the sweetest deal of his life at the stroke of midnight.

He loved the way Coral's emotions played out in her eyes, the gratitude in their soft green depths made him smile. She skimmed her hands lovingly over the dress his mother had bought her, and it was easy to see how much she loved the simple dress. It amazed him how the color of her eyes shifted with her mood—it was damned handy if a man was smart enough to pay attention. And Sage Morgan was damned smart. His years of training as a Master meant there had been very little about Coral he hadn't been cataloging for months. Sage knew her eyes flashed a brilliant spring green when she was angry, they turned almost the color of moss when she came, and they were the soft green of the southern Caribbean Sea when she was lost in the emotion of a moment.

Sage thought back to last summer's Founder's Day festival—he'd watched her from the sidelines and seen the joy in her expression. Each time a child waved his or her small hand in greeting, Coral's eyes had turned this same shade of soft green. For a woman who'd kept most of the adult population in their small mountain town at arm's length, she had sure as hell connected with the kids. Christ, he couldn't wait to watch her flat belly bloom with his child. His mother had already made several less than subtle remarks about becoming a grandmother, and the odds of that ending anytime soon were somewhere between slim and none.

Laughing to himself at the detour his thoughts had taken, Sage brought himself back to the moment. Hell, he had to admit the dress was fucking perfect. Sage owed his mom a huge thank you for picking something so well suited for the lovely young woman standing in front of the suite's pedestal mirror. The dress was sexy, but also classy—it wasn't something she'd feel self-conscious wearing—but damned if it didn't make him hard just looking at the way it hugged her form.

She'd pinned up her long hair, leaving curled tendrils along the sides framing her face perfectly. The back of her slender neck was one of her most sensitive spots. He'd made that particular discovery late last night while exploring every sweet inch of her. She was too slender—something he planned to rectify soon enough, but it didn't do anything to detract from the sweet curves making the dress look like it had been tailor made for her.

Seeing Coral framed in the ornate mirror he'd inherited from his sweet granny made his heart swell. But the depth of emotion—the connection, was one he hadn't expected to experience for years. Knowing there was a piece of his heritage playing a part in tonight's plan made it even more special. When she raised her eyes, her gaze locked with his, the softness in her eyes drew him in like a magnet to steel. The oak mirror was one of the few things he'd claimed after his beloved granny passed, but he'd never dreamed it would become such a treasure until this moment.

He knew he made an imposing figure, framed by the doorway with the hallway behind him, Sage was relieved when he saw her sweet smile. Coral's eyes went wide before her cheeks flushed a deep rose, and he knew she was embarrassed he'd caught her admiring herself in the mirror. He had plans to help her "unlearn" all those feelings of insecurity and self-consciousness, but that wasn't what tonight was about. Tonight was about new beginnings and promises for the future.

Giving her what he hoped was an appreciative smile, he spoke softly, "You are stunning, love." He walked up behind her and looked over shoulder, taking in her entire appearance in the mirror. "It's perfect. As usual, my mom's taste is impeccable." Placing his hands along the sides of her neck, Sage let his palms skim over shoulders before trailing down her arms. Once he reached the tips of her fingers he moved his palms to cup her hips. Giving her a quick squeeze he reversed his path. Sliding his hands up over her hourglass figure made him itch to pull the pretty dress right back off of her so he could spend the next several hours indulging himself in her sweet body. He hadn't seen what was in the plastic bag Mama Morgan handed her as she'd run up the curved split log stairway, but he would have bet it was something very special designed to take his breath away—and he'd been right.

"I can't wait to unwrap this package. Unless I'm missing my bet, my mother also picked up something very sexy you're hiding under this lovely dress. It didn't escape my attention that she handed you two bags, and she knows exactly how Morgan men think." *And isn't that an understatement of mammoth proportions?* The truth was he recognized the logo of the high-end lingerie store in Bozeman. Hell, you might know his mom would find a way to get the merchandise flown in overnight.

"But, your outfit needs just a little something extra, I think." She didn't take her eyes off his as he pulled the gold chain from his pocket. "Keep your eyes on mine, pet." Her gaze never wandered as he pulled the first of his gifts from his jacket pocket. Reaching around her, Sage settled the beautiful piece around her neck before securing the small catch and trailing kisses along the back of her exposed neck.

The three different colors of gold links forming the fine chain gave the piece a rich look and he couldn't wait to tell her the significance of the gold his jeweler had used. Sage had shown Zach Pell candid shots he'd taken of Coral hoping to inspire a unique creation, and his friend had risen to the challenge in a big way. Zach had gone on and on, raving about how the depth of colors he planned to use would bring out the warm colors of her skin tone and highlights of her hair and truthfully, Zach's words hadn't meant much to him. But, now? Oh, yes indeed—his old college pal was an absolute fucking genius. No wonder his store in New York City's jewelry district attracted clientele from all over the world.

Trailing the tips of his fingers along the gentle slope of her shoulder, Sage thought back over the long weeks he'd spent each summer as a teenager working in the mines found on several of his parents' ranches. God he'd hated being stuck underground when his friends and brothers had been enjoying the beautiful Montana summers. But his dad had insisted he learn about the mines from the ground—or underground—up, and damned if the old man hadn't been right. Sage had been able to successfully navigate delicate contract negotiations and resolve conflicts with the rank and file on more than one occasion because he actually understood the workers' concerns.

Before leaving home that first summer his mom pulled him aside and suggested he stash a few nuggets of gold from the various mines each year. She'd promised the two of them would design something together sometime in the future. He'd done exactly as she'd suggested, but he hadn't used a single piece of his stash until he'd decided to make Coral Williams his.

A few months after meeting her, Sage had flown to New York City to meet with his friend from college. The man he'd known for years jumped at the chance to use the box of raw gold Sage had collected. Zachary Pell was the only man Sage would have ever have trusted with, what at today's prices, was an exorbitant amount of pure gold. Over the next couple of months his friend had sent him design options and updates, but the finished products was even more stunning than Sage could have ever imagined.

The chain was supposed to hold a pendant molded in a perfect replica of the Morgan Ranch brand. Their brand was a fusion of a Rocky Mountain skyline and the letter M, and Zach had done a spectacular job of recreating the symbol in gold. But that beautiful bauble was still sitting in the velvet box tucked safely in the vault hidden in his downstairs office. Instead of the pendant—tonight the slender woven chain held a ring. The engagement ring Sage planned to slip on her finger as the old year faded to new was another one-of-a-kind creation showcasing an enormous princess cut diamond.

Sage knew his parents were planning to host a huge engagement party in a couple of weeks, but he wanted to begin the New Year secure in the knowledge she'd agreed to be his. When she saw what he'd placed around her neck, he heard her gasp in surprise. Sage turned her in his arms and pressed his finger against her lips. "Shhhh. Don't say anything yet. Just be patient. This evening is going to be full of surprises."

CORAL'S HEAD WAS still swimming as she and Sage made their way down the winding stairs into the Morgan's cavernous front hall. The gift he'd given her upstairs had stolen her breath but her attention was quickly diverted as they were surrounded by family and friends. The festivities were already in full swing and before long she'd forgotten about the beautiful promise dangling from an exquisite gold chain around her neck.

She couldn't remember a time when she had enjoyed a party more than she had the Morgan's New Year's Eve celebration. Of course on the rare occasions her parents had hosted a party, she certainly hadn't enjoyed any of the festivities. Once she'd gotten a little older, Coral would sneak out at the first opportunity. Both her mom and dad had considered her an "asset" at parties, her job had been to distract the "marks" who'd been invited, giving her parents time to fleece the drunks for anything valuable they'd been naïve enough to bring along. Everything Rob and Jen Williams had done was as shallow as Dean and Patsy Morgan were genuine.

The party was a huge success and Sage had been right, it had been filled with surprises including Charlotte's impromptu karaoke solo of Shania Twain's, *Any Man of Mine*, which had nearly brought the house down around the holiday revelers. Several times during the evening, Sage had pulled small, often very expensive gifts from his pockets...diamond earrings, a slender gold chain bracelet, and an intricate fold filigree barrette for her hair. "You can't keep giving me gifts you know."

"Why not? I missed Christmas with you, and I love seeing you smile. Besides, you heard my mom...you're my girl. And I can buy gifts for my girl if I want to—I know it's true because I hear mom remind dad about that very thing all the time." He'd tried to act indignant, but his grin had given him away. Coral loved this playful side of Sage. When they'd first met she thought he was entirely too somber, but over the past few months it seemed as if something in him had lightened. In her fantasies, his change was because of her, but no one needed to tell her how arrogant and naïve those dreams were.

Coral looked up at the man who was spoiling her shamelessly. "But how did you do all of this? You were here all day and the only brother I didn't see was Brandt and he doesn't even like me." They'd been dancing and she hadn't really meant to speak the last part aloud, but he'd obviously heard her whispered words. Sage leaned back, studying her face for long seconds.

"Come with me." He grabbed her hand and pulled her through the other dancers like the place was on fire. Damn, she was having trouble keeping up and kept tripping over her own feet. *And THIS is why I don't wear heels.* When they finally came to a halt, she looked up into Brandt's stern expression and instinctively took a step back. "Brandt, does that reaction tell you anything?" His expression didn't change much but she saw a muscle in his jaw tense. "Do you know Coral thinks you don't like her? Where do you suppose she got such an idea?"

Brandt's chin dropped to his chest, and she heard his softly muttered "fuck" before he grabbed her hand and off she went again, but this time she was being led her down a hallway. When he finally stopped, Brandt opened the door to a room Coral realized she hadn't been in before and she froze at the threshold. "Shit. I'm sorry Coral, please come in. This is our mom's garden room. I'd like to speak with you in private and I promise to behave." His voice was softer, much more like the one he used when he talked to Charlotte, and Coral noted the hesitance in his tone. *Did he think I'd kick up a fuss and embarrass them all by not cooperating?*

The room they'd entered wasn't huge, but its wall of windows provided a beautiful view of the twinkling lights decorating the elaborate backyard behind the Morgan's home. Coral could only imagine how beautiful the view would be in the daylight...the majesty of the Rocky Mountains laying out in the background would be spectacular. She made a mental note to ask Patsy to see it sometime before remembering the elder Morgans didn't live at the ranch any longer. *I wonder what Sage uses this room for now?*

Stepping hesitantly into the room, Coral was relieved to see Sage enter behind her. He leaned back against the closed door, his arms crossed over his chest. "Hurry up brother, it's almost midnight. And you know I want Coral in the living room..." Coral was getting more confused by the minute but Brandt nodded in apparent understanding. *I swear sometimes my whole life feels like I'm walking from one movie theatre to the next without figuring out the plotline before I have to shuffle into the next theater.*

The rest of the Morgan's beautiful mansion had obviously been decorated with men in mind, the rich colors and a strong western influence made it perfect for its position in the foothills of the Rocky Mountains. But this room was obviously meant to be a refuge for a feminine soul. The overstuffed sofas were a floral print that reminded Coral of a Monet print she'd seen once in a museum gift shop. Pale yellow and delicate blue made the entire room seem peaceful—as if stress wasn't allowed passed its lovely French doors. She looked to the side where Sage stood guard, and he smiled at her as if he understood how much she appreciated the setting.

Returning her attention to Brandt, Coral was surprised to see the regret in eyes that usually held such varying measures of suspicion. "I am sincerely sorry I have given you the impression I don't like you, Coral, although I'll admit I was more than a little frustrated to learn you were in enough trouble to have a *go bag*, yet you hadn't mentioned anything to me." *Oh shit.* Judging by Sage's growl, Coral had a feeling he knew exactly what Brandt had been talking about. "But to say I don't like you is actually a hundred and eighty degrees out. I can't tell you how impressed I am with your courage and honesty. I know I didn't appear to believe you the other evening, but in fact I was already convinced you were telling the truth. The questions I asked were the ones I know you'll both be facing in the future. You'll likely have to answer them all again when you give your deposition—something I'll delay as long as possible by the way. We've been chasing leads on those two idiots who broke into your apartment, but so far they're still in the wind."

When she started to speak, Brandt help up his hand halting her words. "It's my job to read your body language,

Coral. Everything about you speaks of your honesty and sincerity. And I'd already done my homework, sweetheart. I already knew about your background." She wasn't sure if she should be impressed or pissed. Why on earth had he checked on her? "I can almost hear your mind spinning with questions. Just remember, we take care of each other here in Pine Creek—and Morgans damned sure take care of each other. I knew my brother was interested in you and I was trying to make sure he didn't get hurt again."

Coral was surprised to see a break in his usual calm presence as he rubbed his hand through his short hair in frustration. "I swear those two patsies who broke into your apartment are living proof no one should ever trade luck for talent. If we can ever catch up with them, I'm betting they sing like canaries to cop a plea on the burglary charge. Florida has issued a warrant for Sanders based on my report, but I don't hold much hope they've located him yet. From what I heard your ex has risen up the ranks of the local drug trade quickly and that means he probably has more than one law enforcement official watching his back. I'm damned frustrated we haven't been able to do more, and I'm embarrassed it came across as being something personal against you. Hell, we can all see how great you've been for Sage, he's actually been growing more tolerable over the past few months. He almost smiled at a couple of the hands earlier today." He took a deep breath before smiling, and even though she knew he was waiting for her to respond, his smile surprised her so much she almost forgot everything he'd just said.

"You should smile more often, Brandt." She almost laughed out loud at his stunned expression. She surprised him even more by wrapping her arms around him and hugging him tight. "Thank you for everything you're doing, but most of all, thank you for believing me. I may make mistakes, but I don't lie about them. And I was embarrassed to my toes the other night when I had to tell you all that story." Even now she could feel her face burning with embarrassment.

Sage's voice sounded from right beside her, "Okay, that's enough touching…get your own woman, little brother." He wrapped his hand around her wrist and pulled her back into his arms. "Come on, love it's almost midnight and we don't want to miss the fun."

## Chapter Fifteen

SAGE KNEW HE was practically dragging Coral back to the living room but he'd heard the one-minute call several seconds ago and he wasn't missing this opportunity. Quickly making his way to stand in front of the living room's large rock fireplace, he spun her into his arms sealing his lips over hers in a fierce kiss as his brothers closed ranks around them. Phoenix took his position directly behind her, unclasping the beautiful gold chain she was wearing with such dexterity Sage was sure she didn't even realize it was gone. Of course he was doing a pretty good job of distracting her, even if he did say so himself.

Keeping his hands along the sides of her face he kept her focus on him as he pulled back just enough to look in her eyes. Phoenix had been waiting to catch the ring and Sage felt it being slipped into his pocket. *Damn it's great to have brothers...most of the time.* As the final countdown started he retrieved the ring from his pocket. Holding her left hand in his hands he knelt down on one knee.

"Coral, I wanted this to be the first thing you heard in the new year..." And as jubilation erupted around them he slipped the ring on her finger—it was there and there it would stay. He might be planning to *ask*, but there wasn't a chance in hell he was taking no for an answer. "Will you share your life with me? Will you be my wife, the mother of my children, and my partner in all things?" Sage wasn't sure if all the celebration was because the clock was chiming midnight or because of his proposal, but he was straining to hear her answer.

Coral stared at him for several gut wrenchingly long seconds before her eyes filled with unshed tears, and she struggled to pull him to his feet before launching herself into his arms. Peppering his face with kisses, she nodded quickly. "Yes!" The applause around them was so loud he worried his mother's prized crystal bells would start rattling off nearby shelves. Coral had buried her face in his neck, her arms wrapped around him so tight he wasn't even able to take a deep breath, but he didn't care. *Tiny, but mighty strong—inside and out.* "I know it seems fast, love. But, I knew you were the one that first day in the hardware store."

She grinned at him through her tears, casting knowing looks all around them. "Everybody knew didn't they? I kept wondering why no one asked about the necklace, but they all knew already."

"Yep. I'm fairly certain you were the only person within fifty miles that *didn't* know. Hell, mom has been in a flurry since she met you last spring. And by the way, she is in seventh heaven hoping to fill both the mother of the bride *and* mother of the groom roles so be forewarned." He'd barely gotten his words out before they were surrounded by well-wishers, but he kept her tucked safely under his arm so she didn't get swept away in the chaos.

Shaking hands and accepting congratulations, Sage was basking in the glow of a newly engaged man when he locked gazes with the one woman he'd hoped to never see again. Mackenzie Leigh's eyes were filled with malevolence and he could practically feel the frost forming between them. For a second Sage could have sworn he'd been looking into the eyes of a human being who had no soul at all. He knew she cared nothing about anyone but herself, but what he'd seen then was something much more sinister than a woman who thought the entire world revolved around her.

The dark look he'd gotten a brief glimpse of was masked quickly before Mackenzie stormed from the room. Sage hadn't missed the fact she already dialing her phone as she stepped out into the kitchen. Great, just what he needed—her alerting the Bitch Brigade. Hell, her choice of friends should have been sufficient to scare him off. When his parents surrounded Coral, Sage slipped away. Heading down the short hallway leading to his office, he hoped to find his brothers. Giving them a heads up to Mackenzie's presence might help minimize any damage the vicious bitch might cause.

Before he'd found his brothers, Sage felt cool fingers wrap around his wrist, tugging him until he turned to face her. "Dance with me, lover." When he glared at the place where her hand now lay over his arm, Sage felt a wave of revulsion. No wonder Brandt had been so baffled at Sage's interest in her. He could still remember the arguments they'd had late one night out by the barn—it had been the first time they'd physically fought since they'd been kids. Brandt's years as a Navy SEAL meant he was far better prepared for the altercation than Sage had been. He'd known the only reason he hadn't had his ass handed to him was because Brandt hadn't actually wanted to hurt him. *Yeah, and wasn't that a fucking humbling moment?*

"One last dance can't hurt. Surely you don't want to embarrass your family by causing a scene. I just want to say goodbye." The voice he'd once imagined hearing for the rest of his life now made the hair stand up on the back of his neck. By the time they'd returned to the open area where other couples were dancing, the music changed and Sage knew immediately this was just another in Mackenzie's long list of manipulations. The sultry strains of Elvis Presley's *You Were Always on My Mind* filled the room, and Sage tried desperately to tune out the woman pressing her fake breasts against his chest. She recited all the reasons they would be perfect together. *So…a bitch AND delusional. Just fucking perfect.*

Looking across the crowded room, Sage met Coral's gaze. Her crestfallen expression felt like a kick to his gut. Her eyes were devoid of anything resembling happiness—there was nothing but bleak recognition. In that moment he was just another in a long list of people who'd let her down. He'd managed to ruin what should have been the most romantic night of her entire life—Christ, could he have screwed this up any worse?

There wasn't a doubt in his mind this was exactly what Mackenzie had in mind when she'd pulled him out on to the dance floor. Everything with Mackenzie was about winning—it didn't matter if she actually wanted to prize, as long as she won. Everyone had always assumed Sage had been the prize, but he knew better—ultimately it had been the Morgan name, social connections, and money. Sage had been little more than a means to the end.

He watched as Coral turned to speak briefly to Colt, who was staring daggers at him from her side, before she quietly walked away. She kept her head held high but it was easy to see the change in her posture. It was going to be a fucking miracle if one of his brothers didn't shoot him before the night was through. He broke away from the viperous bitch who was still chattering in a voice Phoenix had likened to fingernails on a chalkboard. He didn't offer her any explanation, he simply walked away. Making his way to Colt, he asked, "What did she say to you?"

Colt didn't even look at him. "That she recognized the song from some movie about witches—and how appropriate it seemed." Colt shook his head before leveling a look at him meant to convey exactly how disgusted he was with his older brother. "You're a dick. Coral didn't deserve that, Sage. What the fuck were you thinking, man?" Shaking his head, his brother turned and walked away in frustration. *I've got news for you brother—no one is more disgusted with me than I am with myself.*

CORAL GRABBED ONE of the men's jackets hanging on one of many hooks beside the door before exiting the Morgan's large laundry area and stepping outside. Muttering to herself about the bitch dancing with Sage, she'd tacked on a blistering curse about the snow. *"Fucking fat frog-legged bitch. No wonder she's been so hateful to me when she was in the store. Why didn't Charlotte tell me who she was for heaven's sake? Damn these shoes are even worse in the snow than my sneakers. I don't know why I thought this would work. I don't belong here—that's easy to see. Well, it was fun while it lasted…but it's time to move on. I'm going someplace warm…with a beach…and drinks with little umbrellas in them. Fuckidy fuck it's cold out here.*

Making her way over to the wooden bridge spanning one of the backyard's water features, Coral felt her shoes begin to slip and slide on the snow-covered surface. *Great, with my luck and lack of grace I'll probably fall off this kiddy bridge and break my damned neck.* Wishing she'd taken the time to find a warmer coat, Coral pulled the light jacket's hood up in an attempt to block the frigid wind slicing like a knife against her exposed skin.

The woman Sage had plastered against him had been a mystery to her until the moment she'd seen them together on the dance floor. *At least now I know the score.* She'd often wondered why a woman she didn't even know had developed such an intense hatred for her—as it turned it, her anger hadn't been about Coral at all.

Looking around she realized she'd walked further from the house than she'd planned and now stood well outside the area illuminated behind the main house. Coral had always cursed her complete lack of any sense of direction, she'd learned at an early age to memorize landmarks whenever she traveled. She even jotted down the row and exit numbers when she shopped to avoid wandering aimlessly in the lot looking for her car. She was quickly losing her sense of direction, it was snowing harder now than it had been just a few minutes earlier, and the wind was whipping up what had already fallen. She was struggling to put one foot in front of the other and she was starting to panic as the lights of the house disappeared from view.

There was a brief lull in the wind allowing her to see a faint glimmer of light she assumed was the house and she started to move in that direction. She was getting tired and the frigid temperatures were quickly taking a toll. The light seemed to be getting brighter faster than she felt like she was moving, but she heard the locals talk about how quickly mental confusion set in when the body was exposed to extreme cold. *Yeah, like I needed another excuse for mental confusion. Just think about the beach…nice warm sand, margaritas served by a hot cabana boy.* Cursing her damned imagination for putting Sage's face on the man setting a drink down beside her, Coral tried to focus on making him look like anyone else, but it wasn't working.

*Typical...just fucking typical. I've somehow managed to submarine my own fantasy. Damn, I don't remember the house making that noise.* Lights blinded her for an instant before the darkness felt so warm and inviting she decided to close her eyes for a quick minute before trudging back to the house. She needed to get her things and head out before the roads closed...*yeah, I'll rest for a second and then I'll get moving again.*

SAGE QUICKLY ENLISTED help from his pissed off brothers sending them out to search different areas of the house when he hadn't found Coral himself. They'd all vowed retribution on her behalf, and he didn't doubt for a minute what they would dish out would pale in comparison to what his mom would have to say. Sage was beginning to panic as he paced the kitchen when the young woman who worked in the local drug store stepped in front of him. He'd seen Coral eating lunch with the pretty redhead several times over the past few months, and he'd heard the two had become friends. "Are you looking for Coral?"

"Yes, have you seen her?"

Looking like she wasn't entirely sure she wanted to tell him what she knew, he saw her look nervously to his left. Brandt was standing beside him, his younger brother shook his head letting Sage know he hadn't found Coral upstairs. "Joelle, if you know where Coral is we'd appreciate your help. Even though it may not look like it right now, I assure you my brother does love her very much."

Sage flinched at the truth of his brother's words but

didn't take his eyes off the pretty woman whose attention was now focused entirely on Brandt. *Interesting.* "I saw her walk that way after she saw you dancing with the woman who has been so mean to her at the store. Why did you do that? That bitch has treated Coral horribly for months. Of all the women here—why her?"

*What the fuck? Mackenzie was the woman Coral had been referring to when she'd told them about a woman being rude to her? Why hadn't Charlotte said anything to him?* Sage might have taken offense at the young woman's tone, but deep down he admired her loyalty to Coral.

Setting aside all the questions swirling through his mind, Sage vowed to ask Charlotte why she'd kept this bit of information to herself. Thanking Joelle for her help, Sage headed down the hall leading to the laundry. Phoenix's voice sounded from behind him, "My jacket isn't on the peg. Fuck, that thing isn't going to keep her warm in this weather." Sage pulled open the door and felt his heart sink when he saw faint footprints in the snow—they were quickly filling in with blowing snow so their odds of tracking her were diminishing with each passing moment. "Shit, I'll get help." Phoenix had obviously seen the prints and come to the same conclusion.

As Sage pulled a parka and gloves from a nearby closet his phone rang. Looking at the screen he was surprised to see the call was from the ranch hand he knew had volunteered to check the heifers in the north pasture during the night. He was tempted to send the call to voicemail, but a sudden sense of foreboding had him answering, "What's wrong, Ronnie?"

He could barely hear over the roar of the snowmobile the man was riding, "Boss, I was headed back to the bunk house when I thought I saw something at the edge of the trees about a half mile behind the house." Sage gritted his teeth, Ronnie wasn't usually the type to call him to chitchat about nonsense, why tonight? "Mr. Morgan, cover my ass with Miss Patsy because I'm coming right up to the back door. ETA five minutes." Everyone knew how his mom felt about anyone driving on her precious patio and Ronnie's words sent ice racing through Sage's veins. "Man, I don't know why Miss Coral was out here dressed like this, but she's in bad shape. If Doc Slow is still there you better round him up. And boss, thank your mama for insisting we carry blankets in our emergency packs." The call disconnected and Sage felt his knees fold out from under him—Phoenix caught him with a loud curse shocking him back to awareness.

Moving to the French doors leading to the open area of the patio, Sage heard Brandt barking orders behind him, but his focus was zeroed in on the approaching lights shining through the snow. He was practically growling with impatience even though he was sure Ronnie's painstakingly slow pace was an effort to shield his passenger as much as possible from the icy wind. When the snowmobile was fully in view, Sage could see the real reason he'd been moving at a fucking snail's pace. Coral was wrapped in blankets from head to toe and Ronnie was holding her cradled in front of him—obviously she hadn't been capable of holding on and Sage felt his hope she was alright fading quickly.

The large snowmobile hadn't even come to a complete stop when he stepped forward and pulled Coral into his arms. "Thanks, man." Ronnie nodded, but it was easy to see he wasn't happy about finding her outside in this weather. He might be young, but Ronnie wasn't a fool. It didn't take a rocket scientist to know there weren't many reasons a woman would do something this reckless—and being hurt by a foolish man was at the top of the short list.

BRANDT WATCHED HIS brother sprint upstairs with his woman in his arms as Doc followed as close behind as the aging medical practitioner's arthritic knees would carry him. Brandt had put in a call to his old SEAL team trying to track down his cousin hoping to persuade him to give their small town a shot if he ever decided to finish medical school. After he'd been forwarded several times, Brandt learned Ryan was currently finishing up his residency. He'd already talked to his mom and she'd agreed to speak to Ryan's mom as soon as possible. Watching Doc gingerly make his way up the stairs, Brandt made a mental note to remind his mom to make the call—they were going to be without a local doctor before long if they didn't start making plans.

Brandt looked back at the man who'd likely saved Coral's life and smiled. "Ronnie, go ahead and get this put away then come on back up here as soon as you can. I'd like to get your report before you forget any of the details."

The young man nodded, then hesitated before restarting the machine. Brandt simply raised a brown in question. "I'll come back straight away, but make sure you cover me with Miss Patsy." Brandt held back his smile, seemed his mother's rules about driving on the patio had been passed along to all the ranch employees—Mama Morgan could be a force of nature when crossed so he understood the man's concern.

"Don't worry—you're going to get a pass on this one, she's crazy about Coral. You saved her future daughter-in-law, she's likely submitting your sainthood application as we speak. She'll have all sorts of goodies lined up for you by the time you get back." Brandt wanted to laugh at the look of relief on the younger man's face as he fired up the snowmobile's roaring motor and moved slowly off the large pavers before racing back to the machine shed. Stepping back inside, he noticed Joelle Freemont wedged in a small corner of their large kitchen, her dove gray eyes darting around the crowded room. *Christ, she looks like a frightened animal who's been cornered by predators.*

Joelle fascinated him, there was something elusive about the pretty young woman who worked at the local pharmacy, but he hadn't been able to get close enough to her to figure it out. She was a puzzle he longed to master— just thinking about the shy raven-haired beauty and *Mastering* sent a rush of blood to his groin. *Great. Sporting wood is not going to win me any points, that's for certain.* Before he could make his way to her, Brandt heard Kip's voice from down the hall, "What the fuck are you up to, Mackenzie? Why are you even here?"

Deciding the unmistakable anger in his youngest brother's voice probably merited an intervention, Brandt turned his attention from the pretty woman he'd been watching for months. When he reached the door of Sage's office, Mackenzie Leigh's shrill voice filled the air and Brandt fought the urge to turn around. *Fuck me—everything about that lying bitch makes me want to choke her. I should just leave Kip to it and then help him dispose of the body. Hell, being a brother needs to trump being Sheriff, and besides—this would be a fucking public service.*

"You just mind your own damned business, Kip Morgan. I assure you, Sage was dancing with me because he *wanted to*. What was between us isn't finished." Yes, indeed—he'd help Kip hide her body without a backwards glance.

Stepping into the room, Brandt closed the door before leaning back against it, crossing his arms over his chest in a pose of pure dominance. Hell, he knew he intimidated most people, but he rarely did it intentionally. But, he wasn't going to give the raving bitch, trying in vain to stare down the youngest Morgan brother, an inch leeway. "You weren't invited to this party, Mackenzie. What made you think you'd be welcome?"

She'd evidently been so focused on Kip, she hadn't noticed him until he'd spoken. Turning on her heel, she rolled her eyes. *What I wouldn't give to administer the punishment you deserve.* "Oh goodie, look who else thinks I give a rat's ass what he thinks. Be on your way, Brandt, no one cares about a former SEAL who couldn't cut it with his team so he ran home to play cops and robbers in the boonies."

Brandt didn't care about her opinion—but he wasn't completely immune to her comments either. One look at Kip and Brandt knew he needed to take control of the situation. He wasn't sure he'd ever seen that particular look on his brother's face before, and God only knew how often the four oldest Morgan brothers had tortured their youngest sibling. Stepping forward he made an effort to keep his tone level, "I'm going to escort you to the door now. And for the record, I'm speaking as the Sheriff when I tell you, don't return. Stay away from this family and that includes Coral Williams."

Brushing past him, she sneered, "She's not going to be an obstacle for me much longer. And you'll need to accept my role in Sage's life soon enough." She slammed the door behind her and Brandt was left staring after her wondering how so much evil could lurk behind such a lovely face.

Kip slammed his fist down on Sage's massive desk and growled, "She's a demon. I swear to God she has to be Satan's sister." *Hope he isn't expecting an argument from me!* "And what did she mean Coral wasn't going to be an obstacle for long?"

Brandt shook his head. "I was just wondering the same thing myself."

## Chapter Sixteen

CORAL WORK UP to the sound of hushed voices nearby and was glad she hadn't opened her eyes. She recognized the gravelly voice of Pine Creek's only physician and wanted to groan in embarrassment as her memory started filling in the blanks. How in heaven's name was she ever going to explain her decision to go outside when she obviously hadn't been dressed for the conditions? Sage had already chided her for lack of adequate winter clothing, of course it didn't actually matter now that she'd decided to move on. *No sense buying snow boots and parkas for the beach.*

Sage might not have seen her at the beginning of his dance with the blonde bitty, but Coral had certainly seen the two of them. The woman looked perfectly comfortable in his arms. She'd smiled at Coral letting everyone around them know she was right where she intended to stay. The look of smug satisfaction on the woman's face made Coral want to rip her in two, but ultimately it had been the soft smile on Sage's face when his eyes met hers that had crushed her. He looked perfectly at ease with the woman she could only assume was his ex. And the fact she'd been invited to this party told Coral the woman would likely continue to be a thorn in her side if she stayed—*hell's bells there's no future in that!*

"You can open your eyes now, he's gone." The doctor's voice startled Coral out of her musings and she slowly opened her eyes wondering how he'd know she was awake.

The older man chuckled. "Don't look so surprised, young lady. I've been a doctor for so long I'll bet you could find Moses' vaccine record in my files somewhere if you looked hard enough. Being able to tell when a patient is playing possum to avoid a confrontation is child's play to an old fart like me." When she started to sit up, he placed his wrinkled hand on her shoulder to still her movements.

"Just stay where you are for a minute, let's give your blood a chance to circulate back into your fingers and toes before I check you over. Sage can just stew outside in the hall for a few minutes—it'll do the boy some good to worry over how badly he's messed this up. I swear, I've never known him to make such a monumental error in judgment."

Coral blinked up at the older man in surprise—*damn, I didn't see that one coming*. She would have bet everyone would consider Belligerent Barbie a better fit in Sage's world. As much as she hated to admit it, the two had looked stunning together. Coral wasn't ever going to look that polished, it just wasn't who she was—and she'd learned years ago trying to fit her square-peg self into a round-peg world was a waste of energy and effort.

"You need to wipe that defeated look off your pretty face, dear. Charlotte told me the gal Sage dated has been giving you fits, but honey you got no competition there despite how it looked out on the dance floor. Sage walked away from that heathen all on his own. Don't you read too much into that dance, I'll bet in the end you're going to find out you saw exactly what that scheming demon wanted you to see." Coral wasn't entirely convinced the man knew what he was talking about, but she appreciated his effort to console her.

"Now, let's get you checked out before that man tears the hall apart." Leaning close he whispered conspiratorially, "I'm giving Patsy a chance to have a little chat with her eldest. Damn, I love her fire—she can be hell on wheels when one of her brood messes up. Didn't matter those boys all passed her up before they were out of grade school, she never let a little thing like height keep her from running a tight ship."

It didn't take the doctor long to pronounce her "fit as a fiddle," but he'd also warned her to take things easy for a day or two. "If I'm fine, why do I need to take it easy?"

"Your body has used up a lot of resources and pushing your luck now would likely be too much for fate to resist." Coral understood tempting fate better than most people, so maybe she'd just go back to her apartment and rest there for a few days before heading out. She owed Charlotte an explanation, as well. Sighing to herself, Coral relaxed back against the pillows he'd piled up against the headboard for her. Vowing to rest her eyes for just a couple of minutes before she started gathering her things and finding her car, Coral let her eyelids flutter closed. *It won't hurt to wait until everyone clears out downstairs. No sense in doing a modified walk of shame in front of the whole damned town.*

SAGE SAT IN his favorite wingback chair watching Coral sleep. He'd pulled the chair close to the bed when she'd started talking in her sleep, he hadn't wanted to miss the opportunity to learn more about the woman who'd stolen his heart. The same woman he'd come much too close to losing a few hours earlier. Doc had assured him she would be fine, but Sage was sure he'd never forget how icy her skin had felt and its blue tinge had been terrifying.

He'd spent the past few hours wondering how he'd managed to fuck up so thoroughly. Hell, his own mother was so mad at him she'd refused to even look at him until his dad eventually managed to calm her down. "Don't think this means you're in the clear with me, son. I just don't like seeing your mama so upset—besides, she isn't getting first dibs on you." The conversation with the man he admired most in the entire world had gone south from that point—rapidly. And as hard as the criticism had been to hear, Sage had known he had it all coming.

His brothers had relayed the information they'd gotten from Ronnie. Sage knew there was no way he'd ever be able to convey his gratitude to the man who'd saved her life, but it didn't mean he wouldn't try. Ironically it seemed her new engagement ring had probably been a huge factor in her rescue. Ronnie said a small twinkle of light at the edge of the trees caught his eye and when he turned the snowmobile in that direction, he could see her holding her hand up trying to block the snow from her face. The irony hadn't been lost on Sage.

Listening to her restless mumblings wasn't doing anything to ease his guilt. How she'd thought he was besotted with Mackenzie mystified him, but he damned well planned to clear things up as soon as she woke up. Kip and Brandt had filled him in on their conversation with Mackenzie and he trusted their instincts—if his brothers believed the woman might have plans to hurt Coral, then it was definitely worth investigating. Phoenix had been leaning back against the kitchen counter listening and shaking his head.

"You guys know it's always about money with Mackenzie—we need to follow the money. She's smart, but I'm smarter." Phoenix had pushed away from the counter, snagged several energy drinks from the fridge, and disappeared into his computer lab.

Much to his surprise, the only person who hadn't given him hell was Charlotte. Coral's friend and employer had assured him the storm would blow over quickly. "She's quite smitten with you, I don't think she'll be able to leave—even if she thinks she should. Our girl hasn't ever had anybody she could trust—she needs to know her heart is safe with you." In typical Charlotte fashion, she'd managed to reassure him and still send a camouflaged message. He'd understood and planned to use the information to his advantage.

Leaning forward with his forearms resting on his knees, Sage clasped his hands and stared at the floor. He'd been sitting for so long his muscles were rioting in protest. Exhaling a deep breath, he wondered aloud yet again at his ability to hurt the one woman he'd sell his soul to protect.

"It's okay, Sage. I understand."

Jumping to his feet, Sage moved to the bed, sitting close by her side and pulling her left hand into his. "Actually, I don't think you understand at all, pet. I think we were both manipulated last night, but the blame falls squarely on my shoulders." He shook his head and tightened his grip when she tried to pull her hand from between his. Even all these hours later her fingers were cool to the touch, but nothing like the frigid flesh he'd uncovered hours ago when he'd first laid her on the bed.

"First of all, I want to apologize for ruining what was supposed to be one of the most romantic and joyful evenings of our lives. If I live to be a hundred years old, I'll still regret how things ended last night. My complete lack of consideration for your feelings will haunt me forever. Seeing the hurt in your eyes felt like a knife being plunged straight into my heart." He saw her eyes fill with tears, but he wasn't finished so he forged ahead, "I'll have to spend the rest of my life making absolutely certain you don't regret giving me a second chance, because there isn't a chance in hell I'm letting you go. I know you think you're leaving—hell, I can see it in your eyes even now. But, baby, you're mine and I'll tie you to the fucking bed if I have to."

Tears streamed down her wind-burned cheeks, catching small rays of light in the dimly lit room. Sage doubted she realized how long she'd slept, and he was glad she was awake now. "Come with me, Pet. I have something I want to show you." Wrapping her in a blanket, he picked her up and stepped close to the balcony windows. When he set her on her feet, he saw her eyes widen in surprise. "Before you make a decision about leaving, I want you take a long look at everything being laid at your feet. Look closely, my love because God has painted a personal invitation for you to stay." He moved behind her, wrapping his arms around her and just enjoyed the feeling of her in his embrace.

Knowing his dad's penchant for details, Sage didn't doubt for a minute he'd deliberately positioned the master suite to offer views as any in the world. The afternoon sun was just dipping behind the mountains painting the sky in golden shades of amber and the darker hues of orange and red. Before long the colors would cool to violet before settling into a deep midnight blue bedazzled by millions of brilliant diamonds. Even as a child, Sage had known he'd never be able to leave Montana, the sky alone anchored him to the only home he'd ever known. The mountains and valleys might be a feast for the eyes, but the Montana sky fed his soul.

"I don't want to go, but I'm afraid to stay. You're everything I've always dreamed of, and even though losing you now will hurt...losing you later will destroy me." There was a part of Sage that was proud of her—damn she'd laid it right out there. He was humbled by the fact there was still a part of her that trusted him enough to let herself be vulnerable. The Dom in him surged to the surface, but this time it was all about nurturing her transparency.

"Your heart is safe with me, love. It will always be safe. I'm not saying I won't make mistakes—because I will. But the one thing you can rely on above all else is the fact I'd never intentionally hurt you." The most beguiling green eyes he'd ever seen searched his own dark eyes, her gaze so intent Sage knew she was trying to see into his soul. He sent up a silent prayer to whoever might be listening—*please let her see the love in my heart, the sincerity of my pledge, and depth of my soul's desire to join with hers.*

CORAL LOOKED DEEP into Sage's eyes, pleased to see nothing but sincerity. Growing up surrounded by deceit had trained her well, she'd prided herself on her uncanny ability to spot deceit in others...that is until she'd fallen in with Donny Sanders. Her ex-boyfriend hadn't made her any promises beyond a safe place to stay, but knowing she'd misjudged his character had shaken her confidence. How could she be certain she wasn't making the same mistake this time? How could she be sure her heart would always be safe?

During her conversation with Josie, her sweet friend

had asked if she had a man in her life. When Coral hesitated, Josie had laughed. "I'll take that as a yes…and either he is sitting nearby or you're holding back to protect your heart." Josie had always been intuitive and Coral hadn't been surprised how quickly she'd read her emotions. "I promise to come see you soon, I think we could both benefit from a long overdue movie marathon and margarita night. But until then, please stop holding on to all those pesky insecurities about your parents. Take a chance, you can't soar sitting on the ledge. Take it from a person who's made a career of taking risks—even though some of those have been more beneficial than others." Josie's giggle let Coral know she'd have plenty of entertaining stories to share.

They'd made plans to call one another again soon and as strange as it might sound, it was Josie's encouragement that made all the difference now. Typical, Josie…her ability to pre-empt fate had always amazed Coral. She took a deep breath and decided to take a leap of faith. "I love you, Sage. In a lot of ways it feels like I've loved you forever, even though for so long it seemed like you were only a creation of my imagination." She shook her head when he started to speak, she needed to finish or she might never find the courage again.

"But I'm warning you, I'm stronger than I look. In just a couple of days you've shown me parts of myself I'd never known existed, and I won't sell myself short again. I deserve a man whose heart belongs only to me."

Sage nodded before he pulled her into his arms. Pressed against his chest she found comfort in the warmth of his embrace and the steady beat of his heart beneath her ear. Coral was self-aware enough to recognize her deep seeded need to feel safe. Sage had pushed her too close to the edge last night. She wanted to believe he wouldn't hurt her, but rebuilding the tenuous trust would take time.

"I can almost feel you pulling back and it's killing me, but I've got no one to blame but myself. I've never lied to you—and I won't start now. I don't know why Mackenzie was here, heaven knows she wasn't invited, nor was she welcome. My entire family detests her—hell, Kip was almost apocalyptic and Brandt vowed to help him hide her body should she come near you again."

She was so surprised she pulled back, blinking up at him in surprise. "Oh, pet, you have no idea how protective they're going to be of you. They love you already, it's nothing short of a miracle I'm still allowed in the house. I shudder to think of the digital hell Phoenix will rain down on her." He shrugged nonchalantly before continuing, "But all things considered, she's brought it all on herself."

"She's not a nice person—not at all. What did you see in her?" Coral was genuinely curious since the two of them seemed so different. She couldn't imagine how Sage could be attracted to them both.

"No she isn't nice, but she was very good at masking it for a long time. Honestly? I might have seen it sooner, but I was too stubborn to listen to my brothers. I was so used to being the *big brother* I'd failed to notice they'd all become my equal. Instead of listening and seeing things from their point of view I dug my heels in, refusing to concede I might have made a mistake. It wasn't until I realized Brandt had been willing to sacrifice our relationship to save me from her that I finally came to my senses."

Coral could tell the conversation was painful for him…but the pain didn't stem from the fact he'd lost a woman he thought he'd loved. This was the anguish of a man who'd nearly walked away from a member of his own family because he'd refused to admit he was wrong. She couldn't imagine how difficult it had to be for a man as successful as Sage Morgan to admit he'd made such a huge mistake in judgment. And suddenly she realized how familiar his story sounded. She'd done the same thing with Donny. She'd accepted a second date despite the fact she hadn't really enjoyed his company in large part because one of the girls she'd worked with had warned her against him. It had been her own stubborn pride that led her into a life-threatening situation—*hell's bells and cottontails, we have more in common than I thought.*

It was unreasonable for Coral to hold Sage to a high standard she hadn't been able to meet herself. She'd always prided herself on not being a hypocrite, and judging him when he hadn't judged her for her mistakes would be hypocritical to be sure. Realizing she'd made her decision, Coral wiggled out from beneath the covers to settle in his lap. "Let's rewind to the moment when you said all those sweet things to me and slid this beautiful ring on my finger. I didn't even get an engagement kiss."

She could feel his shoulders relax as he enfolded her in his embrace and smiled. "I'll be happy to correct the oversight, pet. But first I want to warn you—your new brothers are planning to take you to task for endangering your sweet self. I know you didn't have any siblings growing up, but you are definitely getting thrown in the deep end of this pool, love." Coral knew he'd wanted to say more, but she was tired of talking so she decided to take matters in her own hands. Leaning up, she pressed her lips against his. Wrapping her arms around his neck trying to plaster herself against him, the cotton of his shirt brushing against her tight nipples reminded her of the disparity in their states of dress.

"Why are you dressed and I'm not? It's not fair." She'd only pulled back far enough so she would speak the words before slanting her mouth over his again. Even though she was controlling the kiss, she knew it wouldn't last long. He was letting her play but she knew his need for control in the bedroom was bubbling beneath the surface. Their tongues stroked one another in a slow seduction reminding her of all the stories she heard in high school about couples necking under the stars. She smiled against his lips and then wanted to groan when he pulled back looking at her in question.

"Care to share what's got you smiling while I'm trying my best to seduce you?" Sage sounded amused and she was relieved he hadn't taken offense at her distraction.

"I was thinking about all the times I listened to my friends talking about their necking sessions under the stars—and I realized I'd love to do that with you." When he didn't comment, she started to worry she'd sounded like a lovesick teenager.

Using his thumb to brush the worry lines between her brows he smiled. "So much worry, pet. I love hearing about things you're anxious for us to do together. Remember, your passion feeds mine. I want to hear everything…and I hope to fulfill all of your dreams, even those you haven't had yet."

# Chapter Seventeen

*Five Weeks Later*

CORAL STILL COULDN'T believe how much her life had changed in such a short period of time. All of the excitement during the New Year's Eve party fed the local gossip train for a couple of weeks before it finally settled down. Charlotte swore her business had practically doubled as people used any excuse they could to visit the store and chat about Coral's narrow escape from old man winter. She'd been scolded by many, coddled by most and been given so many coats and boots she'd already made donations to two nearby charities.

After Donny was arrested, she'd made the trip to Georgia to give her deposition. The information she'd given backed up the taped confessions Brandt had wrung out of the two men he'd finally arrested several days after the party. Sage made the trip with her and the authorities down south even allowed him to sit beside her, lending his moral support while she'd answered all of their questions as openly and honestly as she could.

She'd hugged Brandt when they'd returned home and thanked him for preparing her so well, before smacking him on the arm warning him that being right all the time was an annoying trait. Sage, Colt, Phoenix, and Kip had all groaned, telling her not "feed the beast" of Brandt's ego.

Brandt had just smiled and kissed her on the forehead before whispering, "Don't listen to them sweet sister-to-be, you just keep on telling me that and maybe someday the *real* Brandt will come home."

His words nearly shredded her composure, but they'd also given her hope that maybe...just maybe, he was on the road to healing. She'd always felt a deep sense of gratitude for every veteran's military service, and wished the government would do more to help those returning home. She'd been sending up prayers that Brandt found the peace he deserved. And after seeing him chatting with Joelle over lunch today, Coral wondered if her sweet friend might be just what Brandt needed.

The wedding was planned down to a gnat's ass and would take place at the ranch on Valentine's Day. Coral had been disappointed Josie's tour schedule was going to keep her from attending, but she'd also understood. God above, she was proud of her friend—as a kid, Josie had lived and breathed music, it was the core of who she was. During their last phone conversation, Coral detected a note of fatigue in her voice and reminded Josie she could always visit if she needed a break.

Damn, it was great to have Josie back in her life, and she could hardly wait to introduce her to Tobi West. Coral and Tobi had bonded immediately during their Facetime calls, what was supposed to be one call had turned into several over the past few weeks, and Coral was looking forward to meeting the tiny blonde dynamo in person. "Make Sage stop by here on your way back from the honeymoon. I'll round up the Pussy Posse and we'll have a margarita night." Coral heard a man shout her name from off-screen and Tobi's grin told Coral she'd made the outrageous statement intentionally. Winking at Coral,

Tobi said, "I gotta go, Kyle's eye is twitching. I might have gone a little over the line with that one. Later!" Coral hadn't even able to disconnect the call she'd been laughing so hard. *That woman is good for my soul.*

For the first time in her life, Valentine's Day was going to mean more than a day of torture when she was forced to watch friends and co-workers receive romantic gifts and listen as they recounted the special dates and dinners their significant others had planned to celebrate. Now she'd have every reason to celebrate the holiday dedicated to love and romance. The past five weeks had been the happiest of Coral's life. She was settling into her new life on the Morgan Ranch, she'd helped Patsy with the wedding plans when she could, truthfully none of the pretty trappings meant anything to her. As long as she and Sage ended up married, everything else was just a bonus.

Coral smiled to herself as she put away the last of the freight that had arrived at the hardware store that morning. God, she loved this little store, its wide variety of merchandise and eccentric owner somehow managed to make each day different from the one before. She had been shocked to learn Charlotte wasn't the struggling small business owner she'd always assumed her to be. Sage had spilled the beans one evening during dinner and the other four Morgan brothers had howled with laughter when they'd heard how she'd worried about the older woman. *Rat bastards.*

She'd been ecstatic when Charlotte had agreed to be her Matron of Honor, having the feisty seventy-three year old as her only attendant was going to make their wedding even more special. Coral stood up straight, arching backward in an attempt to work out the kinks in her back, strong hands spanned her waist. She'd been so startled she almost dropped the box-cutter she was holding. Coral had never liked being scared, anyone jumping out from behind doors to frighten her usually got punched before she even realized she'd reacted. It looked like she was going to have to remind Sage again. "Hey, lover, did you forget? I really don't like being scared like this." She had barely spoken the words when the hands tightened so tightly she knew she'd have bruises from the punishing grip.

"I don't give a rat's ass what you like, bitch." Coral felt as if her blood had suddenly been replaced with ice. She'd prayed she would never hear his voice again and knowing Donny Sanders was in the store terrified her. "Don't make a sound—not one. Did you think I wouldn't make bail? Or that I couldn't find you myself? Although I have to admit, that the blonde bimbo Mackenzie, saved me a lot of time." *Blonde bimbo? Sage's ex helped Donny find me?* Her mind was scrambling trying to fit the pieces of the puzzle together. How on earth had Mackenzie Leigh connected with Donny?

As his hands tightened even more at her hips, Coral sucked in a deep breath to keep from crying out. She was determined to deny him the satisfaction of knowing how much he was hurting her. Movement in the small decorative mirror above her caught her eye. Coral blinked in surprise as Charlotte peered around the sights of her hunting rifle. Her elderly boss grinned before she winked. Coral knew Charlotte and her husband had been accomplished hunters because the evidence was all over town. Their mounts were displayed in many of the local businesses, Charlotte had regaled her with dozens of hunting stories.

Coral saw Charlotte mouth the words, "on three drop," and she steeled herself for what was about to happen. Donny leaned over her shoulder and sneered,

"You know if I kill you I'll walk right? Those jerks that rolled on me will never live to testify, and their confessions aren't shit now that my lawyer knows you're fucking the Sheriff's brother." The vehemence in his voice assured her he had no qualms about eliminating anyone who stood in his way. How had she ever fooled herself into thinking she was safe with him? Why hadn't she trusted her instincts?

"Now turn around and walk your ass right out the front door and maybe…just maybe, I won't kill the old bat you work for." His words made her breath catch, just thinking about how she'd endangered the people around her threatened to make her knees fold out from under her. Before she'd taken a step, she saw Charlotte mouth three, Coral tried to spin quickly to dislodge his hold so she could drop, but his grasp was too tight. Something in her mind snapped, a blazing hot fear for not only herself, but for Charlotte too, sent the world around her spinning wildly out of control as pure rage filled her.

Coral slashed him with the box cutter she still held, his fingers released just enough of their vice-like grip she was able to drop to the century-old wood plank floor. Before her mind even registered the cool boards pressing against her cheek the room was filled with the deafening crack and the world seemed to explode in a shower of shattered crystal. Gasping, Coral's mind was clouding quickly as she tried to pull in oxygen, but the black edges of her vision were closing in so quickly she finally surrendered, letting it carry her into a warm, peaceful abyss.

SAGE WAS AT the diner with Brandt when his brother received Charlotte's text. *Help!* That one word was enough to send them both into a blind panic. Charlotte had never asked for help—*ever*, and knowing that one word had been all she'd had time to send spoke volumes. In the short time it had taken them to run the half block to the small hardware store Sage was certain each step he took forward moved him further from his goal.

His fear for Coral was unlike anything he'd ever experienced. *Fuck, when did the diner and hardware store move so damned far from one another?* Before they reached the small store, the unmistakable crack of a rifle filled the air. A blinding rage filled Sage causing him to stumble, he was grateful for Brandt's quick reflexes. His brother had fisted the back of his jacket keeping him from going down face first. "Christ Sage, keep your feet under you, man." *Not all of us trained in the Special Forces, little brother. Some of us are mere mortals.*

Bursting through the front door, Sage sucked in a breath—it looked like a small bomb had gone off. Sage was certain his heart had stopped when he saw Coral crumpled on the floor next to a screaming man he knew was Donny Sanders. The sewage spewing from the man was enough to make a sailor blush. Brandt stepped close to Sanders yanking him to his feet before hauling him away from Coral. All Sage heard was Brant's growled, "I don't give a shit about your shoulder. Suck it up and shut the fuck up before I shoot you myself." Before they disappeared around the corner, Sage heard Brandt bark, "Why the fuck did you just wing him, Charlotte? Christ you've never missed a hit." *Hit?*

"Wasn't my fault. He didn't let her go and he jerked when she cut him. Did you hear all that whining? Christ, it's just a wing-shot. What a pussy." Sage might have found Charlotte's frustration funny if he hadn't been so worried about Coral. "I could have gotten him with a second shot...but, those are harder to explain, Brant, you know that." He'd checked Coral's pulse, sagging in relief when it pounded steadily beneath his fingers. Sage shook his head at Charlotte's antics as he started pulling the larger pieces of broken crystal from her hair, and gently brushing smaller pieces from her face.

By the time Sage stood up cradling Coral in his arms, he could hear the sirens approaching and he sighed in relief. Charlotte's voice sounded from beside him, "She's alright, you know. I don't hit anything I ain't aiming for...although I did intend to hit *him* a bit more *centered* if you know what I mean." She'd jerked her head in Sanders direction, still looking disgusted at the way the man was complaining. Returning her attention to them, Charlotte looked down at Coral and smiled, "But that ornery girl got all pissy when he said something about hurting me, and she sliced him with the box-cutter." He could hear the admiration in Charlotte's voice. She shook her head, "Ass hat jerked to the side at the last second—dang it."

Sage looked down at Charlotte, the woman he'd known all his life and had always considered tough as nails, was standing there with big tears in her eyes. When he grinned at her she shrugged, "What can I say? I really wanna be in that wedding, and I wasn't about to let that pile of roach crap screw it up." She'd waved toward the front of the store where Sanders was slumped on the floor—completely silent, blood pouring from his nose. Sage wanted to laugh out loud—obviously Brandt had gotten tired of listening the prick's ranting and administered a little knuckle anesthetic. Looking back down at Charlotte, her wrinkled fingers were softly tracing along the side of Coral's pale face. "Besides, she's my girl. And I wasn't letting him leave here with her that was for sure."

Sage was relieved to see Coral's eyelids flutter open. She looked up at him, but he was sure she hadn't actually *seen him*. His relief was short-lived when she started thrashing in his arms as if she was being pursued by the devil himself. She obviously hadn't registered *who* was holding her, but his barked command to *"Stop!"* stilled her. Coral's eyes finally focused on his face, but the recognition was followed by a flash of fear.

"Charlotte? Where is Charlotte? Oh my God, is she alright?" That was his Coral, always thinking of someone else first. He set her on the front counter, but didn't take his hands off her. He blocked her view of the paramedics wheeling Sanders out to the waiting ambulance, and hoped Brandt could stem the flow of people pouring into the store until Coral was more settled. He knew she was in shock and she wouldn't want to be that vulnerable in public.

"Sweetness, Charlotte is just fine. She is right over there talking to Brandt." He tried to step to her side, but she clung to him like a frightened child. He wasn't about to deny her or himself the comfort of cuddling her against his chest despite a second set of paramedics' attempts to assess her for injuries.

"He was going to kill me but I saw Charlotte with a big-ass gun in the reflection of a mirror, and she said to drop on three, but his hands were so tight I couldn't drop, and he said Mackenzie helped him, and he told me he'd kill Charlotte if I didn't go with him quietly…and I didn't want him to hurt Charlotte…I didn't care about Mackenzie…she's vile…but then, well, I got so mad I sort of lost it and I cut him and he let go and I dropped and then I heard a loud crack, like lightning hitting right beside me and glass went everywhere." Honest to God, Sage had no clue how she'd managed to say it all without taking a single breath. *Incredible.*

Laughter sounded from next to him, Sage looked up into Colt's smiling face. "Holy shit sweetness, that was damned impressive. I'm thinkin' it might have even been some sort of world record." He looked to his right nodding his head. "Look over there. Now this is really is going to be entertaining. Brandt is trying to take Charlotte's rifle in as evidence. She has a big bear hunt planned for the week after the wedding and she isn't going to up her prized Marlin 4570 without a fight." Colt stepped closer and leaning closer to Coral, kissed her forehead before whispering, "She probably has a dozen of 'em, but just you watch—she's going to swear this is her one and only." Coral's lips curved up at the corners and Sage was grateful for Colt's insight. He'd seen a way to diffuse Coral's escalating stress, and it had worked perfectly.

Neither he, nor Colt had missed Coral's comment about Mackenzie, but before he could question her about it, Phoenix and Kip came running through the front door. Both men scanned the small group of people and Sage saw them both sag in relief when they saw Coral. Phoenix surprised everyone by being the first to reach her and pulling her off the counter and into his arms. Holding her tight against his chest, he breathed out, "Oh little one, don't you ever scare me like that again or I swear I'll paddle you myself. I always wanted a sister and I'm not giving you up, you got that?" The rest of the Morgan brothers stood by in stunned disbelief as the least dominant of them transformed into Uber-Dom right before their eyes. When Phoenix looked up as he handed her off to Kip, he shrugged. "She needs to take better care of herself. I like her and I don't like very many people, okay?"

Sage heard a giggle and looked at Coral to see her eyes fill with tears despite the soft laughter beginning to surface. Kip gave her a quick hug and moved her right back into Sage's arms. Brandt leaned over studying her closely before nodding to him. "Adrenaline crash in fifteen. You better get her home quick."

Sage didn't need to be told twice. He tossed his keys to Kip and simply said, "Let's go." One of his youngest brother's claims to fame was his need for speed and he didn't disappoint—they made it home in record time. Within minutes Sage managed to carry her inside, strip them both, and get into the shower. Coral had called it an oasis, he'd seen her retreat into the rock and plant lined enclosure when she'd needed to relax. It was the obvious choice now when he needed her mind as settled as possible before her body bottomed out.

Massaging her tight shoulder muscles he thought back to the moment of terror he'd felt when he heard the unmistakable crack of a rifle. And seeing her crumbled form lying on the floor had nearly given him a heart attack. *God, if you're listening—thank you for keeping her safe, but holy hell, please don't ever do that to me again.*

Pulling her close he wondered if he'd ever be able to let her out of his sight again. He heard her sniff, but this time he was actually relieved to see her tears because it meant she was still engaged emotionally. Brandt had sent him numerous texts while they'd been driving home detailing she signs and symptoms of an adrenaline crash, so Sage knew what he was seeing was normal and all things considered she was holding up remarkably well. Sage shook his head, hell, his little brother acted like he didn't have a lick of sense—the texts from Brandt had been so detailed it had almost been like reading from a "Medical

Issues for Dummies." *Talk about overkill.* But he also understood it had been Brandt's way of looking out for Coral when he couldn't actually be at the house with them.

Turning her around, he looked down at her and smiled. God, her eyes were impossibly large and filled with so many competing emotions Sage wondered if he was really equipped to help her navigate the troubled waters ahead.

"Just love me. That's all I need from you Sage. I just need you to love the memory away."

Sage's knees almost buckled at her soft words, but he managed to stay focused on the woman standing before him. Realization slammed into him full force—it was the *only thing* she'd ever asked of him. All she had *EVER* wanted was to be loved. There wasn't anything in the world he wouldn't have been willing to buy for her, nothing would ever have been too much...yet all she'd wanted was his love. Leaning down, he pressed a kiss against her forehead, "Well, my love, I can certainly do that."

CORAL FELT SAGE'S hands moving over every inch of her body with such deliberation she wondered if he was trying to memorize each contour and curve as she lie spread out on their bed. And then she recognized what he was doing...this was about his need to reassure himself she really was okay. She had a few nicks from the broken glass, but nothing requiring stitches and a very few small cuts that had even needed bandages.

Every stroke of his hands fueled the burning need building inside her, it was if his touch alone could light up her body from the inside sending spears of desire from her heart to every single one of her erogenous zones. All of her fears melted into need as he stoked the fires of passion. Soon the only thought in her mind was her overwhelming desire to feel his hard cock sliding deep inside her.

Coral didn't even try to hold back her moans and sighs, his touch was the perfect distraction. When she finally started begging with words, he positioned himself above her staring into her eyes. "You scared ten years off my life today, baby. I would love to make slow sweet love to you, but the truth is I don't think I can. I'm going to fuck you hard and fast because I need to find a way to expend all this pent up energy. And I need to feel you shatter in my arms."

He must have seen the recognition in her eyes when she nodded in understanding, it was all the permission he'd needed. He pushed in just enough to test her readiness. "So wet, always so ready for me." Coral felt her body respond to his words as juices bathed the tip of his cock, easing his way. "Fuck me you are so deliciously wet, love. Your pussy is so hot, you are burning me up, pet." He sank in all the way and she relished the way the bulging veins on his engorged cock stimulated the sensitive walls of her sheath. She was looking forward to learning more about the D/s lifestyle, she was particularly looking forward to her first visit to one of the clubs she'd heard him talk about. But right now, all she wanted was to surrender herself into his care. Her body was his to command. Coral was surprised at the huge sense of relief she felt once she let everything go and put herself completely into his care.

She knew the sexual Dominant in Sage would sense her surrender, it would sooth the desperation he felt to know without any doubt she was indeed safe. Her needs were much simpler—she simply wanted to feel safe wrapped in his arms. She needed to give herself to him—to let him control this moment, but most of all she needed to feel loved and cherished. Pushing all the day's stress aside, Coral forced all of the fear to the back of her mind and vowed to simply *live in this moment.*

BRANDT STARED AT his phone completely stunned by the text he's just received. *Ask Sanders about connection to Mac.* Surely Sage wasn't serious—Brandt couldn't imagine how the two of most disgusting and vile people he knew could have managed to connect with one another. He started to tap out a response questioning his brother's sanity until he remembered hearing through the grapevine that Mackenzie had dated a sheriff's deputy in Denver. Had she used the connection to gather information on Coral? It was certainly possible. Hell, he'd gotten a lot of information pretty easily so he knew it could be done—and Mackenzie would have been highly motivated if she saw her meal-ticket slipping away. Brandt had never believed Mackenzie Leigh had given up on marrying Sage, but this would be a new low—even for *her.*

Donny Sander's shoulder wound was superficial and he'd been treated and released quickly from the local hospital. Brandt leaned back in his chair and stared at the small screen monitoring the jail's newest resident's cell. Shaking his head in disbelief, Brandt typed in the commands to record both sound and video—perhaps Mr. Sanders would be in the mood to chat.

## Chapter Eighteen

STANDING AT THE top of the stairs, Coral gasped as she looked down over the beautifully decorated scene in front of her. The banister was wrapped in pine boughs tied with off-white and burgundy bows, the muted white lights twinkling deep in the branches added a sparkle that reminded Coral of the way moonlight seemed to love dancing on the snow covered branches at night. Sage had taken her on a moonlight horseback ride a few nights ago, when he'd pointed it out to her, she'd been mesmerized by the way the trees seemed to shimmer.

Stepping off the last step of the split log staircase, Coral smiled when she noticed her path was illuminated by winding parallel rows of tiny flameless candles. The message wasn't lost on her, Sage had made certain she'd be able to find her way to him. Stopping when she reached the edge of the living room, she let her eyes move around the large room. She basked in the glow of what had to be at least a hundred candles, marveling at the way everything seemed to take on a luminescence—it was almost otherworldly in its beauty.

The soft strains of a piano playing, *From This Moment* faded into the background when her gaze locked with Sage's. His dark eyes flared as his gaze traveled over her body, and she could have sworn she could feel the heat—as if he was actually touching her, and Coral felt her body heat in response. She saw the corners of his lips turn up—he obviously knew exactly what he'd done to her—*rat fink*. Sage was standing in front of the stone fireplace, the mantle beautifully decorated to serve as their alter. He was waiting patiently for her, letting her enjoy every moment of this special evening. His indulgence filled her heart with so much love the tsunami of emotions froze her in place. She couldn't move, God, she could barely breath. As if he understood where her mind had gone, he gave her the sexy half-smile that always made her melt as he held out his hand and mouthed the words, *Come to me, pet*. The simple gesture pulled her back to awareness and before her mind could catch up, her feet were already moving.

Sage's bright white western cut shirt highlighted his tanned skin and dark hair—*God in heaven he's hot and he's mine…all mine!* All four of his brothers stood by his side, dressed in deep burgundy western shirts and dark jeans. Coral hadn't wanted a formal ceremony, preferring something personal that reflected the family's humble way of living their lives. Expensive trappings weren't what made a marriage strong, she'd told Patsy she wanted everyone to leave with wonderful memories not an engraved knick-knack they'd take home and tuck in a drawer.

Charlotte's dress matched the brothers' burgundy shirts, its soft fabric shimmering in the low light. The elderly woman's face opened in a huge smile as Coral approached. Charlotte had grinned unapologetically when Coral confronted her about her financial status. When Coral asked her why she'd kept her in the dark, the ornery woman had actually giggled. "Well, at first I wasn't sure you weren't playing me, and then…well, by the time I got to know you better and knew you were sincere it was too late." Charlotte's eyes had shined with unshed tears and she'd grasped Coral's hand across the table where they'd been enjoying coffee. "After my Walt died, lots of folks thought they'd buddy-up with me because of the money. But you liked me *for me*, not because of the money." Coral was glad she hadn't known, because they'd both needed to know their friendship was genuine.

When she reached the end of the short aisle, Coral turned to kiss and hug Sage's mother and father. They'd been so wonderful to her, making her feel like she was a part of their family from the very beginning. Moving on to Charlotte, she pulled her into a hug and whispered, "Thank you for being my friend. I'll never forget—every blessing, every moment of joy in my future will stem directly from the moment you gave me a safe place to learn how to live…a shelter in the storm where I could find everything I'd ever dreamt of. I'll always be grateful." When she pulled back there were tears streaming down Charlotte's face.

Turning to Sage, she fought the urge to throw herself into his arms. When he looked down into her eyes, Coral practically melted. Those beautiful windows to his soul were filled with a mixture of love, pride, and concern that rocked her to her to the depths of her soul. "Are you okay, love?" When she nodded the first tear of joy escaped to race down her cheek. He leaned forward and kissed it away. "Don't cry, baby."

"These are tears of joy and gratitude. I want to take it all in—I don't want to miss a single moment."

Leaning forward, he kissed the tip of her nose. "I promise to fill your life with precious memories. Now, let's get started on that, shall we?" She nodded and felt a goofy grin move over her face. She listened to the minister's sweet words as he joined them as man and wife, grateful they'd chosen to recite traditional vows. Looking up at Sage, pledging to love him until her last breath filled her with a sense of purpose that made her heart stutter, she'd never made a promise she meant more.

Before the ceremony concluded, Sage leaned forward and pressed a soft kiss to her lips. When he stepped back, she was surprised to see his brothers had formed a semi-circle around them. Colt was the first to step forward, he lifted her hand and clasped a beautiful gold bracelet around her wrist. Holding her hand between his own, he looked down at her and smiled. "This chain represents the links of family and the strength we give each other. None of us are as strong individually as we are together."

Brandt stepped forward next, clipping a small deep coral heart on to the delicate chain. "This heart represents the joy you have brought into our family. You'll be loved and cherished by each of us. You've shown me there is hope...and I'm counting on you to keep pulling me into the light of your healing circle." Coral could feel the tears building. *Darn it, I'm going to bawl like a baby.*

Before Phoenix took her hand he pulled a soft linen handkerchief from his pocket and blotted her tears. His thoughtfulness always humbled her, and she sent up a quick prayer that he found a woman who would cherish that gift. He kissed the back of her hand then added a second coral heart to the bracelet. "My heart is variegated, it means I'm finally emerging from the shadows. Thank you for showing me how easy it is to talk with people if I'll just take a chance." He leaned forward and kissed her forehead. Sage gave him an easy smack upside the head and growled something about finding his own woman, making everyone in the room laugh.

Kip didn't waste any time stepping forward and attaching the light colored heart with darker swirls he'd pulled from his pocket. "My heart represents youth and intensity. Thank you from the bottom of my heart, sweet sister because I am no longer the youngest in the family. *Finally!*" As soon as he stepped back into his place, the room erupted in cheers as she and Sage were introduced as Mrs. And Mrs. Sage Morgan.

SAGE HAD SEEN Coral stop at the top of the stairway and had a moment of panic thinking she might be reconsidering, until he'd noticed the look of wonder on her face. She was taking in everything around her. He thought back on something he'd heard her say several times over the past year and he knew what she was doing...Coral was making a memory as she took in everything around her. That sense of appreciation was one of the many things he loved about her. She'd only ask for one thing during the entire wedding planning process. Coral had heard through the local grapevine that Colt could sing and she'd asked him to sing something special during the reception and dance.

Sage hadn't interfered in their conversation, he'd just leaned back in his chair watching her expertly paint Colt into a corner. "Please, I've heard such wonderful things about your voice, and you know...since Josie can't be here, well...I'd hoped to get the next best thing." He'd wanted to laugh out loud. She'd played the guilt card and the admiration card in one lay-down. Perfect. Telling Colt he was a small step below one of country's hottest stars had been a brilliant play. But in the end it had been Colt's love for Coral that made him concede.

Sage had known how disappointed Coral was her

childhood friend couldn't attend the ceremony. She'd understood, but he'd seen the light in her eyes fade a bit the day she'd found out. He'd been thrilled when Josephine Alta contacted him several days ago asking if she was still welcome. The two of them had put together quite a surprise for his lovely wife. It was almost show time, but for now he was leaning back against the wall watching as she accepted congratulations.

"She's really something, son, you're a lucky man." His dad mirrored his pose, and grinned. "In a lot of ways Coral reminds me of your mama. A kind heart, a willingness to put others before herself, and a fresh way of looking at things even when those around her are jaded." The words seemed odd under the circumstances, and Sage looked over at the man he admired the most in the entire world raising a brow in question. It was unlike his dad to be vague and Sage wondered what was behind his comment. "Don't look so puzzled, boy. I just want you to guard that sweet heart of hers." Nodding in Coral's direction, his dad sighed, "She'll be your greatest asset if you let her. Teach her to follow her heart and she'll bring more joy into your life than you can ever imagine. Treasure each moment—even the ones when you think your patience has been tested beyond its limits, because time slips away very quickly."

Pushing away from the wall, his dad grinned, "Time for me to find my own lovely bride and remind her why she's *my* greatest treasure." His dad waggled his brows making Sage laugh out loud. Before he walked away, his dad looked over at his new daughter-in-law with love in his eyes. "She let your mama plan almost every single detail of this day. The only time she dug in her heels was when she thought we were spending too much."

Sage hugged his dad and grinned. "Pops, she got the

simple wedding she wanted, but I promise I've got a couple of surprises up my sleeve."

His dad laughed. "I'm not sure I've ever seen anyone blush like she did the other night. Make sure the staff at the resort treats her right." His dad slapped him on the shoulder and laughed as he walked away.

Coral may have gotten the simple wedding she'd wanted, but she was getting the honeymoon she deserved. Sage had steadfastly refused to share any of the details with her, simply promising her she was going to be spending a lot of time naked. She'd blushed so deep her ears had practically glowed because they'd been having dinner with his parents at the time. His mother had leaned over and whispered, "Don't be embarrassed, darling. Hopefully it means you're going someplace warm."

Coral's face had brightened immediately at his mother's comment. She was still adjusting to the Montana's harsh winters and he could hardly wait to see her enjoying one of his few indulgences. He'd purchased a beautiful bungalow inside one of his favorite Maldives resorts several years ago. His unit was over the water next to the one his parents had owned for years. The resort's manager had been thrilled to learn they'd be spending their honeymoon there and Sage knew the staff would pull out all the stops to make the love of his life feel welcome.

Their wedding ceremony hadn't been elaborate, Sage appreciated the quiet simplicity with which their lives had been joined. He'd never believed the hype that wealthy people needed to spend lavishly to put their money back into circulation—he preferred to spend it behind the scenes, funding local disadvantaged kids' education was one of his favorites. Looking at the light in Coral's eyes, he could hardly wait to introduce her to the work the Morgan

Foundation was doing with at risk youth. Her background made her a perfect spokesperson—kids would be able to relate to her in a way they rarely could with other adults.

Hearing his brothers' comments during the ceremony made him proud of the men they'd become. He'd been touched when Brandt suggested the addition to the ceremony shortly after they'd become engaged. Sage suspected Coral would always share a special bond with his middle brother simply because they'd hit a bump in the road in the beginning. Phoenix gave him the signal from across the room and Sage began making his way to his bride. Taking her hand in his, Sage grinned down at her. "I have a surprise for you, pet." Pulling a white silk scarf from his pocket, he tied it around her eyes before scooping her up in his arms. When she squeaked in surprise, he laughed. "I don't want you tumbling down the stairs—I have wicked plans for you later, and they don't involve spending any time with Doc."

CORAL WAS GIDDY with excitement as Sage carried her down the stairs and into the large open area near the pool. She could almost feel the energy pulsing nearby as excited whispers surrounded her. Whatever he'd planned had their guests wound up tight. He set her down with her back to the stage where the D.J. was set up. When he removed her blindfold, the grin on his face was pure joy and made her wonder if this was what he looked like a child. She could only imagine how many times this particular grin had gotten him out of trouble. He kissed her sweetly then said, "I'm told this song holds some special memories for you, my love."

She watched Sage nod to someone behind her and the first notes of a familiar song started to play. There was only one person in the whole world who would know the memories tied to *Thank You for Being a Friend*. Coral and Josie had adopted the Golden Girls' theme song years ago. Pretending their hairbrushes were microphones, they'd sung the song hundreds of times before settling in to watch the antics of Betty White and friends. Jumping up and down, Coral screamed as she spun around to see her friend waving her forward.

Josie pulled her on stage and handed her a hairbrush. They sang, laughed, and cried their way through the song before collapsing in a fit of giggles. "I can't believe you're here." Coral felt her eyes fill with tears, she couldn't imagine what it had taken for her friend to change her schedule.

"It killed me to think of missing your wedding…soooo, I made a couple of calls, got Sage's number and I'm here to tell you, that man can move mountains when he wants to…I'm trying to hire him to manage my tour." Coral looked over at Sage, the pink tinge on his cheeks made her want to laugh. Josie still chattered so quickly you had to be paying close attention or you missed big chunks of the conversation. Coral grinned, because her sweet friend was right…Sage was the best thing that had ever happened to her.

Josie sang several of her hits, treating their guests to a private concert unlike any other they'd ever be able to attend. When Josie finally persuaded Colt to join her on stage, everyone in the room felt the magic as their voices blended together seamlessly. It sounded as if they'd been singing together their entire lives. And talk about off-the-chart chemistry—holy shit those two looked seriously hot together.

The rest of the evening passed in a blur. It was the most fun Coral had ever had at a party and everyone around her seemed to be enjoying themselves as well. She danced so much she'd finally kicked her shoes off and continued dancing until she was about to collapse. Brushing back the long tendrils of hair sticking to the sides of her face, she smiled at the youngest of the Morgan brothers. "I have to stop, Kip. I'm done in." When she started to step back, he shook his head and turned her into her husband's waiting arms.

"One more dance, my love. This song is from me to you. I want you to listen carefully to the words, and rest assured each word is exactly what my heart wants to say to yours." When she realized Colt was standing on the small stage singing *Everything I Do* by Bryan Adams, she felt tears fill her eyes. Laying her head over his heart, she let herself melt into the dance. The lyrics whispered to her soul and she knew in that moment her heart was forever bound to his. Their future lay before them in a sparkling panorama and the view was breathtaking.

# Epilogue

BRANDT MORGAN LEANED against the wall watching his new sister-in-law and her friends dance. He couldn't hold back his smile, damn they were having a great time. His personal contribution to the wedding festivities had been the rental fee for several vans and their drivers. The shuttles had picked up many of the wedding guests at their homes and would return them home safely. He hadn't wanted to risk losing any friends on the twisting mountain road leading to the ranch. Driving under the influence was not only illegal, it was dangerous, and preventable.

Brandt watched Joelle Freemont step over to a nearby table to take a gulping drink of her bottled water. When he'd offered to act as her designated driver, she'd shaken her head explaining that she didn't drink and riding with him would be "too dangerous." He wasn't sure she'd intended for him to hear her words, but there wasn't much about her he allowed to slip by unnoticed.

"She's beautiful, but damned spooky, that one." His younger brother Phoenix tipped the top of his beer in Joelle's direction and grinned. "What do you think her story is? Her record is so clean it squeaks." Brand understood exactly what his brother was saying—anything that scrubbed had to be created. *Damn, the Feds usually don't make that sort of mistake—unless they're trying to get someone killed.*

"I have been wondering about that myself, but I'm afraid to ask too many questions. I don't want to draw attention to her if she has a reason to hide, and I don't want to spook her either." If she ran, he knew he'd never find her and there was something about her that drew him in. Hell, she was the first woman he'd been interested in since he'd moved home. Oh, he'd dated and he'd topped subs at the kink clubs he visited, but Joelle was the first woman he'd wanted to spend time with when they weren't both naked.

"She's way smarter than she wants anyone to know." Brandt raised a brow in Phoenix's direction in question. "It's in the way she speaks, the way she puts words together. Listen closely and you'll hear it." *God damned Mensa brother.* Why hadn't Brandt noticed that? *Maybe because you're too busy trying to figure out how to get her into your bed.*

"Word on the street is one of the boys from the Dennison Ranch has taken an interest in Joelle." *What the fuck?* Phoenix nudged him. "Don't sit on your hands too long brother, she's a sweet one even if she's a mystery." His brother stood straight and grinned over at him before moving back to the bar. Brandt stayed in the shadows watching as Joelle darted down the hall to the powder room. The little minx had been avoiding him all evening, but *that* was about to end. Moving to the end of the hall, Brandt stepped to the side and waited.

JOELLE LOOKED INTO the mirror and sighed. Damn that man had been watching her all evening. She'd managed to stay one-step ahead of him, but she suspected her time was running short. Brandt Morgan didn't appear to be a man who would be dissuaded for long. His dark eyes always seemed to be tracking her…like a wolf watching a lamb.

They'd shared a table at the local diner on several occasions and she'd been surprised to discover the normally stoic sheriff was actually fun to talk to. He was well read and had traveled extensively as a Navy SEAL. He'd been as open about his military service as she suspected he could be, and the few times she'd asked something sensitive he'd just shaken his head no without answering. She'd appreciated the fact he hadn't given her that cheesy line about having to kill her if he answered the question. *Wish I had a dollar for every time I've heard that line.*

Brandt Morgan was straight up sex on two legs. The man exuded confidence on every level, but she'd seen flashes of vulnerability in his eyes more than once which made her wonder how many layers lay beneath the swagger. Walking back down the short hall, Joelle couldn't hold back her smile. Holy shit, who'd have ever thought Coral Williams would turn out to be childhood friends with Josephine Alta? Or that the singing sensation would perform at Sage and Coral's wedding celebration?

Joelle had learned years earlier there was nothing to be gained by regret, but seeing Brant's blatant interest in her made her wish things were different. What would it be like to have the freedom to pursue her interest in the local sheriff? Taking a deep breath, Joelle firmed her resolve to resist the temptation he represented. When she stepped back into the room, Joelle gasped in surprise when warm fingers wrapped around her wrist before spinning her against his chest, "Dance with me, minx." *Oh brother….*

## The End

# Books by Avery Gale

## The Wolf Pack Series

Mated – Book One
Fated Magic – Book Two
Tempted by Darkness – Book Three

## Masters of the Prairie Winds Club

Out of the Storm
Saving Grace
Jen's Journey
Bound Treasure
Punishing for Pleasure
Accidental Trifecta
Missionary Position

## The ShadowDance Club

Katarina's Return – Book One
Jenna's Submission – Book Two
Rissa's Recovery – Book Three
Trace & Tori – Book Four
Reborn as Bree – Book Five
Red Clouds Dancing – Book Six
Perfect Picture – Book Seven

**Club Isola**

Capturing Callie – Book One
Healing Holly – Book Two
Claiming Abby – Book Three


I would love to hear from you!

Email:

avery.gale@ymail.com

Website:

www.averygalebooks.com/index.html

Facebook:

facebook.com/avery.gale.3

Instagram:

avery.gale

Twitter:

@avery_gale

Made in the USA
San Bernardino, CA
02 July 2017